Frayed

KARA TERZIS

Published by Sourcebooks Fire, an imprint of Sourcebooks, Inc.
P.O. Box 4410, Naperville, Illinois 60567-4410
(630) 961-3900
Fax: (630) 961-2168
www.sourcebooks.com

Library of Congress Cataloging-in-Publication data is on file with the publisher.

Printed and bound in the United States of America.
VP 10 9 8 7 6 5 4 3 2 1

To my mother and father—
for letting me chase my crazy dream

Dear Kesley,

My therapist tells me I should write you a letter. Every time I see her, she asks whether I've started, and every session, I tell her it's a stupid idea.

But here I am, writing a letter to a dead girl. I tried saying it's morbid, but that ran dry when she said it could be therapeutic. Like flushing all my thoughts and feelings out of my system and onto paper.

I pondered where I should start the letter. Where, after all, did our story begin? From the moment you were born...or died? I chose the latter, thinking that at least the letter would be done quicker that way.

Starting this letter is one of the hardest things I've done. There are so many places I could start, but I chose this place. So here goes nothing, Kesley, because it began—and ended—with you.

And that end began when Rafe Lawrence came back to town...

One

THE UNHEALTHY GROWL OF A CAR PULLED me from my thoughts. I fixed a smile on my face as my best friend, Lia Zhang, pulled up to the curb.

The window slid down with a hum, and she poked her head out. Her long curtain of glossy, black hair had the sleek, model-like look that hair product ads promise. Lia's half-Filipino, half-Chinese heritage also showed in her flawlessness skin.

"Get in," she said. "You must be freezing your ass off out there."

I shivered at her words, just then noticing the way

the cold seemed to bite at my skin, but I ignored the feeling of foreboding that crept up on me. I walked around to the passenger seat and slid in, the warmth from the heater engulfing me. Oddly enough, I didn't find it comforting.

Music pumped from the car speakers, but when Lia saw my gaze flicker toward them, she rolled her eyes and turned it down. She knew I hated music.

"You're ten minutes late," I said. "Why?"

She pressed her lips together before she laughed. "Yeah, I know. Such a rebel, right? 'Cause, like, I have a record of being so punctual anyway." Lia was known for always being late. Fashionably, but still—late was late. Time was precious. It could seep past you without you even knowing.

And then, in the blink of an eye, it could vanish.

I tilted my head in her direction. I knew Lia like I knew the back of my hand. Better, probably. And by the way her eyes were too focused on the road ahead, I knew something was wrong. Then, just like it always did, her calm facade cracked.

"Just don't be angry at me, okay?" she whispered.

"You know I won't," I said, and despite the thick cloud of depression that still covered me, I managed a small smile. Or a replica of what used to be my smile anyway. Most people didn't look deeply enough to see the difference.

Lia shot me a skeptical look but answered. "I ran into someone this morning at the café."

"Who?" I asked.

"Rafe Lawrence."

My mind went blank for a moment as I stared out the window. I was distantly aware of the thumping that was coming from my chest and getting louder and louder as the seconds ticked past. *Breathe, Ava, breathe.*

"Yeah," said Lia. "I know, right? He leaves, and suddenly, a month after Kesley dies—" She broke off with a stiff glance in my direction. "Anyway," she continued, "he's back now. He told me he wants to talk to you." I swallowed, but my throat was dry. It felt like I was swallowing parchment. My tongue felt too thick in my mouth, and I couldn't seem to form words.

"Right," I managed.

"You're not going to go, right?" she said.

I hesitated. Was I?

"Don't be *insane*, Ava. You know the boy has issues. I never understood what Kesley saw in him." Her jaw tightened for a fraction of a second.

"They weren't together like that," I said, cutting

her off swiftly. An instant defensiveness had sprung up inside me.

"If you say so," Lia muttered, eyeing the marked road that stretched ahead of us. "Besides, you know it's not something Jackson would like. He loves you and only wants to see you safe."

I sighed and glanced out the window again. Lia and I were both stubborn; we both thought we were always right. That was where we clashed. Continually. But she was also the best and almost only friend I had, so I clung tightly to her.

She and Jackson were the only ones I had left.

But I also knew Lia had seen Rafe as more than just a friend of Kesley's, something Lia would deny profusely because he'd rejected her on multiple occasions.

I'd always wondered just how bitter she felt toward Kesley about that.

But she was right about Rafe. Jackson *wouldn't* like me meeting him.

The pine trees were a blur of green and brown as we sped past, heading in the general direction of the one high school that Circling Pines had. Winter was drawing closer by the second, though the thought didn't bother me. At least it would give me an excuse to stay indoors all day. Located close to the Rocky

Mountains, Circling Pines fell in the southeastern area of British Columbia, and winters are cold here.

"What exactly did Rafe tell you?" I asked Lia as we passed the only shopping strip—a collection of cafés and overpriced clothing stores.

"Not much," Lia admitted. "Only that he wanted to meet you for coffee this afternoon to talk." There was a pause. A very deliberate, prolonged pause. "I also told him you wouldn't go."

"Lia…"

"I know! I'm sorry! But you can't actually be considering this."

I folded my arms over my chest and glared at the pine trees. My hands shook, and I resisted the urge to ball them into fists. "Until you give me a good reason why I shouldn't go, I'm going," I said in a surprisingly calm voice.

Lia tapped the steering wheel in a melodic sort of way, though I knew it was more a nervous habit than a conscious thought. She seemed to be fighting against saying something, as if she were worried it might upset me. I'd seen that look plenty of times in the past weeks.

"What's bothering you?" I said.

"What do you really know about Rafe?" she blurted out.

"Um. He was a year younger than my sister and spent way too much time in juvenile detention. My foster mother never liked him much—"

"Okay, okay," Lia interrupted. "I mean, what do you know about Rafe and your sister?"

"I don't know. She never told me much about him, all right? Can we just leave it at that?" The school gates were coming into view, wrought iron and impressive looking, with ivy that clung to the metal like a winter coat.

"Fine," Lia said. She angled the car into an open parking space near the back of the almost-full parking lot and killed the engine. The lot was deserted. Everyone must have been in class already, meaning Lia and I were horribly late. She pulled the car keys out of the ignition and stuffed them into her jacket pocket with a brief glance in my direction. "All I'm saying is that your sister was murdered, and there's a killer on the loose."

Her words sent more of a chill through me than the bitterly cold air outside.

———

"Miss Hale, Miss Zhang. For the third time this week, you're late." The clipped voice of my English teacher

came from the front of the classroom. In synchroniza-
tion, every student in the class turned to watch as Lia
and I entered the room. *Almost* every student in the
room, with the exception of one. Rafe Lawrence was
leaning back in his chair, face tilted toward the front
of the room, and looking exactly as I remembered. As
if he had sensed me looking, he suddenly shifted his
gaze to fix on mine. His expression was hard to read,
though I could have sworn his lips curled at the edges
a bit.

I looked away quickly, stomach twisting.

Mrs. York fished something out of her desk and
headed toward us, her high-heeled shoes clipping
against the linoleum floor.

"What's that?" I asked as she handed us each a slip
of paper.

"Detention. For a week. My compassion is wearing
thin, Ava." A hot feeling crashed over me, and I felt
my cheeks blaze with humiliation. I felt a gentle tug
on my shoulder from Lia, and I let her pull me over to
one of the spare seats and sat down heavily, stowing
the detention slip in the depths of my backpack.

"Old bat," Lia muttered in my ear. I allowed a
grudging smile and tuned out for the rest of the
English lesson.

───

"I didn't know Rafe was coming back to school," I told Lia as the final bell rang through the school. Everyone scrambled to gathered up their books, pencils, and other belongings and hurried to leave as quickly as possible. The swell of vague school chatter increased, so I had to raise my voice to be heard over the noise.

Lia shrugged. "Neither did I, but it makes sense. Have you thought about what I told you?"

"About Rafe? Lia, it's coffee. What do you think he's going to do to me?" We left the classroom and headed toward our lockers. At the beginning of the year, we'd switched so we could be beside each other. Otherwise, with lockers assigned alphabetically, Zhang and Hale were pretty much at opposite ends of the corridor. Lia remained silent as I stuffed several books into my backpack without bothering to see if I needed them or not. Something white poked out against the dark blue of the backpack, and I drew it out. It was the detention slip—to be signed by my mother and handed back to my teacher tomorrow morning.

I shoved it back in and shut the locker door harder than necessary.

"This is Rafe we're talking about," Lia said, slamming her own locker shut. "What wouldn't he do? Just call me when you get home, all right? He's waiting for you outside."

"I will," I replied, but I had already turned away. Nerves danced in my stomach, twisting into an anxious knot. I gripped the strap on my backpack harder than usual, feeling how slippery it was with sweat. Why was I so nervous? This was Rafe, someone I had trusted. So why couldn't I shake the feeling of dread? It curled over me in a thick wave as I squinted through the crowd, looking for a familiar pair of blue eyes and dark hair.

Rafe was nowhere to be seen. People looked at me as I passed through the crowd, their eyes filled with fake sympathy or just curiosity. The crowd seemed to part for me, students drawing back against their lockers like I had some highly contagious disease.

I stumbled my way toward the glass doors of the back exit.

I was the sister of that girl who had been murdered, the one they showed on the news every night. People in this town seemed to cling to any news story bigger than an attempted robbery like it was their lifeline.

I broke out into the sunshine with a relieved sigh. The gentle warmth of the sun caressed my skin, and the light wind tugged my hair back behind me. I'd chosen the back entrance of the school, knowing there wouldn't be as many people here. The fewer people there were to stare at me, the better.

A narrow path wound through the trees along the backstreets of Circling Pines. If I took it, it would lead through the backstreets of Circling Pines—past the cemetery and on to the patch of woodland where my house was. The faint echo of traffic sounded in the distance, but apart from that, it was silent. The chatter of schoolkids had cut off as soon as the school's glass doors swung shut.

"Peaceful here, isn't it?" said a voice from behind me.

I turned to see Rafe leaning against the glass doors. His arms were crossed, and he looked comfortable as he gazed at the trees. It wasn't difficult to see what girls saw in Rafe Lawrence, and it wasn't just because of his bad-boy stigma or piercing blue eyes. He had a certain attractiveness—from the sharp, defined angle of his jaw to his curved lips and the dark hair that curled around his ears and above his eyes.

"Yes, it is," I said. Rafe pulled himself off the doors and came to stand close to me. Too close. My fingers tightened on the strap of my backpack, cutting into my skin. "Uh, Lia said you wanted to talk to me?"

"Yeah. She also told me you wouldn't come."

"Sorry about that," I murmured. "Lia can be... protective of me sometimes, you know?"

"Like Kesley."

"I guess," I whispered.

Rafe was watching me carefully, his gaze lingering on the left side of my face.

"How about that coffee?" I said.

Trouble followed Rafe right into Circling Pines.

Circling Pines hasn't changed much since you died. The streets are as quiet as they've always been, despite the tourists that filter through the town on their way to visit the national parks. The mountains still rise on either side of us, and the pine forests continue to grow. I half expected the mountains to come crumbling down when you died or the forests to shrivel up and die.

Rafe and his parents had moved in only a few streets from where we lived with our foster mother, and we spent most of our time together.

Remember when we were seven and eight, and we'd race down the empty streets on our bicycles, leaves scattering in our wakes? Or when we were nine and ten, and we'd fly our kites along the high overlook just east of town?

Or when Rafe and I were twelve, and you were thirteen, and we were beginning to notice things we hadn't before. Like the shape of his jaw and mouth and how he was quickly becoming taller than us, voice deepening.

One moment stuck out like a red petal in snow.

It was the beginning of high school. I was nervous, terrified, and alone. You'd told me you'd meet me at the gates for my first day. You weren't there, but Rafe was.

Rafe looked at me, saw my expression, and said, "You don't always need her, you know. You're smart. And capable. And one day, Kesley might not be there to help you."

I never realized how right he was. Because you never know how much you're relying on someone until they're gone. Until they're swept away without warning, and in a heartbeat, you're alone and left floundering.

I've felt a lot like that after you died.

I didn't just lose a sister and a friend—but a protector too. You were always there for me through thick and thin and everything in between. In third grade when Stacey Miller threw my glasses down the toilet because they looked funny, you made her go out and buy a new pair. That memory was still sharp, and I've been wearing contacts for the past few years. And just a few years later when Amanda Dawson stuck a "Kick Me" sign on my back, you slapped her across the face.

Now that you're gone, Kesley, I have no big sister to protect me...

CHAPTER

Two

TEN MINUTES LATER, RAFE AND I WERE
seated in the one of the many cafés in town, my fingers curled around the hot edges of a coffee cup. The
scent of coffee filled the room, and the warm glow
from the fire that crackled in the fireplace sent dancing
rays of light across our faces.

We hadn't said much on the trip here. Rafe seemed
different than I remembered. Some of the cool confidence that used to ooze from every pore had evaporated, leaving a quieter boy behind. Still, that didn't
stop him from catching the eye of the pretty waitress
and winking at her.

"So you just came back from Vancouver today?"
I asked.

"Yesterday, actually. I figured it would be best—"

"You missed my sister's funeral," I said. My grip
tightened involuntarily around the hot cup; it scorched
my skin, but I hardly noticed. "It was a month ago."

"I know. I... How was it?" he asked quietly.

"Painful."

"I'm sorry."

"Don't be." But my tone suggested otherwise. In a
way, I was absurdly jealous. How was it fair that he'd
skipped past all the pain and the tears and the sleepless
nights leading up to the funeral? And then there was
the funeral itself. I don't remember much of it. It's all
just a blur of tears and words.

I fixed my gaze on the swirling contents of my cup,
remembering all the times I'd ditched first period
with Kesley to have coffee. That would never happen
again. It felt wrong somehow to be sitting here with
her former best friend, talking and having a cup of
coffee. An awkward silence had descended, and Rafe
broke it first.

"Do you ever wonder..." He paused, cleared his
throat, and started again. "Ava, she was murdered—"

"Do I ever wonder who killed her?" I finished for him.

He nodded.

"I wonder that every second of every goddamn day."

"Do they have any idea?"

"No," I said, cutting him off. "They don't know."

"And you're okay with that?"

"Am I *okay* with that?" My mouth popped open in surprise. "Of course I'm not. But what can I do about it? I'm no detective. They told Mom and me they would do their best to find out who..." I couldn't finish the sentence.

Neither could Rafe. He dropped his blue gaze to his own cup. He still hadn't touched it. I stared out the windows at the cars zooming past on the main street and wished I could be anywhere but here. Silence fell between us, interrupted only by the clinking of glasses by the couple at the table next to us and the chiming of the bell every time someone entered or exited the shop.

I stood up abruptly. "I should go—"

"Okay," Rafe agreed, and he rose to his feet too. There was nothing more to say here, I realized. He had only wanted to talk to me because I was *that poor girl whose sister was murdered*. I wondered just how much he cared about me. About Kesley. I was on the verge of asking, but Rafe was already flagging down the waitress to pay for the coffees.

He flipped open his wallet just as the bell chimed and a few more customers walked through the doors, bringing with them a strong, harsh wind. A piece of paper was blown from his wallet and fluttered onto the table. Before Rafe could reach down to pick it up, I did. My curious gaze skimmed across the paper, and I realized a moment later that it was a plane ticket from Vancouver to Calgary. The date read: *September 9.*

Only two days before Kesley died.

I visited your grave every day, even though you wouldn't have wanted me to.

You'd shake back your hair and say, "Gosh, Ava, don't be so morbid!" And a smile would appear on your lips—a sweet, playful smile. Then you'd roll your eyes and saunter away, trying to flip your hair behind you like all the bitchy girls do at school.

The day Rafe came back to school was no exception. The overwhelming need to be close to you, or where you were buried, drove me to the cemetery in an attempt to ease the knot of anxiety in my chest.

I had the way to your grave memorized from the first time I'd come alone.

Your headstone is the prettiest. It's made from white marble that reflects the glistening afternoon sun, with golden, curvy letters marking your date of birth and date of death, and the words "You Will Always Be Loved" carved into the marble.

That day, I reached inside my pocket and placed a rose there that I'd taken from someone's garden on the way. Even though I knew the rose would wither and die in just a few days, seeing it on your headstone made me feel better.

Most days, I didn't know what else to do. So I talked.

I talked about how things have changed, how much Mom and I miss you, how much I've cried when I can't sleep at night. I told you every small, insignificant detail of my school day—what sort of designer bag Lia had brought with her to school and how unfair it was that I received after-school detention. I wondered aloud what you would have said, how you would have reacted.

I told you how Rafe had come back to see me, about how he had enrolled in Circling Pines High School again. Would you have been happy? Upset? Sad? Confused? And finally, I told you about the plane ticket. About the date that was written there. About how I thought...how I thought that maybe he could have been involved with...

It wasn't fair. Any of it.

I stood at your grave, actually considering that your best friend might have killed you and wondering why you were the one who had been killed.

Why not me...

CHAPTER

Three

FOR A PLACE THAT HELD SO MANY TERRIBLE
things, the cemetery was devastatingly beautiful at this
time of the afternoon. I couldn't help but think the
lighting was perfect for painting.

"Ava?"

I glanced around. A familiar-looking figure appeared
from the trees to my right, silhouetted against the
withering light from the sky.

"I'm here," I said, knowing he'd want a reply. My
boyfriend, Jackson Palmer, emerged from the darkness
and came to stand next to me. I wondered briefly
whether he knew about my meeting with Rafe.

"Your mother called me, said she was worried when you didn't come home after school." Jackson moved forward and put his arms around my waist, brushing his mouth against my neck. It felt nice to be able to lean into something solid, something warm and so, so alive.

I sighed. That sounded *exactly* like my foster mother. Ever since Kesley died, she'd been particularly protective. Not that I blamed her.

"Right, yeah." I pressed a hand to my forehead where a dull ache had started up. "Sorry, I forgot to call her and tell her I'd be here."

Jackson frowned.

"What?" I said.

"Nothing. You just look upset. Would you rather be alone?" I thought I detected a hint of bitterness to his voice, as if he thought I didn't need him, but maybe I was imagining it. Jackson was all the boyfriend I needed and wanted, and I was sure he knew that.

I turned farther into the circle of his arms and placed one of my hands on either side of his face, forcing a smile. "No...I just...wanted to see *her*." I felt stupid as soon as the words slipped from my mouth. Was it morbid to find comfort in sitting beside a grave every day?

Maybe Jackson thought so too, because he didn't say anything. To cover the slightly awkward moment, I looped my arm in his and started back up the path of the cemetery. Not exactly a prime location for a romantic stroll.

"How did you even know I come here every afternoon?" I asked.

"I followed you," he said simply.

I felt a slight flicker of irritation, but I pushed it back. He was concerned about me—that was all. Emotion tightened my throat so much that I couldn't speak. I sometimes wondered why Jackson was still with me. Wouldn't it be easier to walk away than deal with the troubled girl who had just lost her sister?

I'd quickly learned not to question my blessings.

We reached the edge of the cemetery, and I stopped to look back. The sun had dipped below the horizon, and a blue-purple gloom had settled over the headstones, reflecting my mood perfectly.

Jackson, who seemed to realize my mood was declining rapidly, said, "Remember that first time we met?"

Almost against my will, I felt a small smile curve my lips.

I said, "How can I forget?"

He laughed, and the sound broke through the eerie

silence of the falling night. "You're right. Seventh-grade camping trip. We hiked up in the middle of nowhere that spring, though it was still pretty cold at night."

"You lent me your jacket," I said. "You said that if I got any colder, I'd turn blue and my toes would fall off."

I turned to face him and saw his hazel eyes crinkle as he smiled. If the truth was told, I had been in love with Jackson from that moment on, but I had been too afraid to show it. We hadn't gotten together until he asked me to the end-of-school-year dance two summers ago.

And we'd been a couple ever since.

"Come on," he said, taking my hand and leading me down the street. "Your mother will be sick with worry by now."

***

He was right about that. My mother yanked me into a tight hug as soon as I unlocked the door, refusing to let me go until I told her I was fine at least five times. Then she pulled away and wiped her eyes. Tears. Guilt tugged at my insides as I realized I wasn't the only one suffering.

We stood in the brightly lit hallway, the white light gleaming off the immaculately cleaned surfaces of the modern house. There was a lot of glass and metal and white tiles that were scrubbed clean as soon as a speck of dirt was visible. The hallway was cavernous, and from where I stood facing the arched doors of the kitchen, the bitter scent of cleaning agents burned my nostrils. Whenever she was under pressure, Mom thought she could just clean the stress away. It rarely worked.

The only room she hadn't touched was Kesley's. Every time I walked down the hallway to my room, I still caught a whiff of jasmine perfume. The scent of sorrow still clung to her room.

"Did Jackson tell you where I was?" I asked.

"I—"

"Mom?"

"Well, he said he had an idea…"

"What exactly did he tell you?"

"Oh, sweetie," my mother whispered. "He said you would be at Kesley's grave."

I flinched. I wished he hadn't told her that. I wished he'd just dropped me at home and I'd made up a story about my cell phone dying while I was studying at the library like a normal person. I felt my mother's hand touch my face. Warm, gentle.

"Sweetheart," she whispered, her voice tender. "Maybe you should see someone about this..."

My face heated, and I shook my head vehemently. I stretched a smile across my face, but it felt fake.

"I have homework I need to do," I whispered, heading up the carpeted stairs. I made sure I looked at the woven material beneath my feet as I walked down the hall to my room. Family pictures of Diana, Kesley, and I hung on the wall, pictures that depicted happy people, pictures that showed a family full of light, where the darkness couldn't touch them.

A family that no longer existed.

A family that had broken apart when Kesley was murdered.

If I had inherited one trait from my birth mother, it was my love of painting. Kesley found her solace in piano, and I found mine in the slashes of paint against an empty canvas.

I'd sit in my room overlooking the road and set up my mother's easel. It was one of the few things I still had left of her—not a memory but a real, tangible object. I'd run my fingers along the wooden edges, thinking, *This is where my mother painted. Drew. Did she think of me when she put paint to canvas?* Since Kesley's death, I hadn't touched the easel. It lay gathering dust in the attic. But today—today was different. The sun seemed to shine a little brighter. The fall leaves looked a little more colorful.

After bringing the easel and paint into my room from the attic, I stared out the window and closed my eyes. Inspiration was a tricky thing. It came and went, just as day and night did. I breathed out a slow, careful sigh.

All I had to do was put paint to canvas. Simple.

I raised the paintbrush, dripping with black paint. And then I started painting.

I lost time as I painted. There was nothing but me and the strokes of paint splashing against the stark white of the canvas. Outside, the sky turned from the pale gray of dusk to the deep blue of twilight. I heard the sounds of my mother downstairs and the hiss of the kettle being turned on. I was completely, utterly tuned in to what was before me—so much so that I didn't even *realize* night had fallen until I couldn't see my own work. I finally rose from where I worked and flicked the light on, sending light across the canvas.

The painting was a tangle of lines. Black, red, dark

green. It was hard to make out any defining images, but if I looked hard enough, I could see the outline of tall pine trees touching the very tips of the canvas. My stomach plummeted. And there, I thought, I could see a lake. The gravel road that usually led to the lake was twistier than in real life, and I had painted it into a texture that resembled rope.

The lake where she was killed, the rope that had strangled her...

What was I *doing*, drawing pictures of Kesley's death scene? Was I becoming like my mother, whose artwork became darker and darker before her end?

My stomach twisted, my throat tight and painful. I snatched a pair of scissors from my desk and tore at the canvas until it became shreds. I didn't want to paint. Never again.

Our foster mother doesn't like me going to the cemetery to visit your grave. Because even where there are good memories, there are bad memories too. And during the dark times, I think a lot about our birth mother. Did you ever wonder what things would have been like if our birth parents were still alive?

Would I be the same broken person I am today? Just how much of that tragedy shaped who I am? I don't remember much of them. Sometimes when I close my eyes and strain my mind, I can catch fleeting glimpses of what were the happiest times of my life.

All I have to remember my birth parents by are the pictures I keep on my desk, but a picture is a picture, not the real thing. My brain has protected me from the painful memories—just like with the acid incident, which was too traumatic for a barely six-year-old girl to cope with. The doctors all told Diana the same thing: the memories were there, locked somewhere in my brain, and I had the power to remember them. So sometimes, late at night, I lie in bed and think. And think. And wait for the memories to come. I know I had walked into the reception of Diana's work. I can still remember

that I was so short at that age that my legs had
hovered a good few inches from the ground when
I sat on one of their chairs. I can remember you,
Kesley, sitting beside me and fiddling with your
hair. We'd been told to wait for our foster mother
in the waiting area and not to venture into the
corridor. But I think I'd grown bored, and you'd
said, "Let's play a game, Ava. Let's do something."
We'd wandered into the corridor, and...

Everything goes blank.

It was ironic though. Not remembering much of
my childhood was supposed to protect me, but it still
hurt, knowing that memories of our birth parents were
locked somewhere in my brain, unable to reach them.

You remembered them, Kesley.

I remember the cold winter nights where we'd sit
in front of the fire, and you'd tell me everything
you remembered about our parents. You told me how
our real mother used to sing to me when I couldn't
sleep. She was a good singer, you told me. She used
to paint too. Sunsets and brightly lit landscapes,
but as her illness grew like darkness within her, her
paintings became darker, more twisted. And our
father, a kind-faced man, balding, with lines like
cobwebs around his eyes when he smiled.

What if my six-year-old self hadn't been late for school? Would our father still have sped down those icy roads? Would he still be alive now?

What if our mother had seen someone about her depression? Would she still have taken her own life or would she be with me now?

And perhaps the most important question of all—would you still be alive...

Four

THE NEXT DAY STARTED BADLY—AND NOT just because it had begun to rain, though that was certainly a factor. A thick fog clung around the house like a veil as I slammed the front door shut on my way out. I was already in a touchy mood after the ten-minute lecture from my mom about receiving detention, which, ironically, was going to make me late for school.

Lia's car was nowhere in sight, and just when I had conceded that I was going to get drenched on the way to school, golden headlights cut through the fog ahead of me. The soft purr of an engine filled the air, so different from the usual growl of Lia's car. I frowned, squinting through the gloom. A moment later, I saw Jackson's face through the tinted windows as the car pulled up neatly to the curb.

I stumbled forward past the rusty, old fence and down the sidewalk until I slid into the passenger side of his car, grateful to be out of the rain.

"Thanks," I said in a voice that sounded like a sigh. "Where's Lia? She usually drives me to school." We'd made that arrangement as soon as Lia didn't have to be supervised while driving.

"At school. She texted me," he said, and for some reason, there was a tightness to his mouth. Though I couldn't imagine why. Fog swirled around the car, obscuring everything except the immediate surroundings. I found it made me anxious, almost claustrophobic, so I looked down at my feet instead. Jackson drove slowly, carefully.

"You're going to be late, you know," I told him.

"I know." And then he smiled. "But my track record of arriving late to school is much cleaner than Lia's, so when she couldn't come, I offered."

"Thanks," I said. We rode the next few minutes in silence.

Jackson took in a sharp breath, as though he had

been about to say something but had thought better of it. His brow was pinched into a scowl as he looked at the road ahead of him.

"Yes?" I prompted, curiosity evident in my voice.

"You know Kesley's old friend is back, don't you?" Instantly, I stiffened in my seat. Even the mention of Rafe made me nervous. I'd managed to forget about the plane ticket for a short time, but Jackson's throw-away comment sent me crashing back to reality. I needed to talk to Rafe to clarify things.

"Old friend?" I picked at some of the dried paint under my nails, feigning disinterest. "Who?"

"You know," said Jackson. "The one with the blue eyes. Ralf or something."

I smiled despite the situation. He would hate being called that. "Rafe. And, no, I didn't know he was back." There was a brief moment of silence before I ventured further. "When did he arrive?"

"A few days ago, I think. That's what he was telling everyone anyway."

My blood turned to ice at Jackson's words, but I made sure that none of the turmoil twisting inside me showed on my face. Rafe was lying when he came back to Circling Pines. What was that supposed to mean— and why? To clear his name or for some other reason?

The plane ticket suggested he came back before Kesley's death—but my sister's funeral had been almost a *month* ago.

"You okay, Ava?"

I swallowed. My throat felt too thick. Mouth too dry. Uncontrollable fear pulsed under my skin, shooting adrenaline through my veins. I had to reach down out of sight and pinch my forearm. The sharp pain helped to clear my mind, helped me think more rationally.

"Yeah, I'm fine." I knew I didn't sound it. "I just… I just didn't realize he was going to come back after Kesley—" I stopped there, biting down hard on my tongue.

"I want you to stay away from him," Jackson said. I was taken aback by the hardened edge to his voice, but I dared to shoot him a look. His face was expressionless enough, although a muscle in his jaw ticked.

"Why?" I asked hesitantly.

"He's bad news. I can feel it." Under any other circumstances, I would have laughed and asked if Jackson was psychic, but the last thing I felt like doing right now was smiling. Instead, I just stared out the window without replying. I was beginning to wonder if Jackson knew something about Rafe that I didn't.

The fog was gradually beginning to float away, and the school's harsh outline was becoming visible through the gloom.

"Just promise me you won't—" Jackson started.

"Okay, okay, I promise. There's no need to sound like my mother. One is enough, thanks." His laughter broke through the tense silence, and I smiled.

Another beat of silence passed before I ventured to speak again. There was something I wanted to know—desperately—but I wasn't sure how to bring it up without making it sound like an accusation. "How's May?"

May, Jackson's older sister and a senior in high school, was the same age as Kesley. Being a junior, I'd always felt intimidated by May and her friends. I regretted asking about May when I saw Jackson's fingers clench around the steering wheel, but he answered me in a relatively calm voice.

"Better than usual, actually." Then he added, "I guess as good as she can ever be. Still doesn't do her homework, and she's probably going to fail her final exams."

"What about...*them?*"

He laughed. "*Them?* Their name isn't cursed, you know. You can say it."

I grimaced. "I know. I just don't like them. I don't get it."

"You and the rest of the town," he muttered.

May was part of Circling Pines's infamous girl gang KARMA. In the past few months alone, their little group had committed more than ten indiscretions at the expense of other people. Usually, these were just small, immature things, like stealing from the local grocery store. Or spray-painting walls. But now and then, something more horrible would crop up. Like an incident a few months ago that left an old woman without her diamond ring and with a very nasty cut over her right eye. Several trips to juvenile detention and many hours of community service later, the girls still hadn't learned their lesson.

"Right," I said, wondering how to phrase the harsh accusations in my head. Did I believe them capable of murder? Stealing, assault, graffiti... That was at one level—but *murder*? What could possibly motivate someone to take another's life?

"Why did you ask then?" Jackson said, hearing the skepticism in my voice.

I turned my head toward him, watching his gaze focused on the road ahead, but his eyes narrowed slightly.

"No reason," I murmured, sinking farther into my seat.

I didn't have the guts to tell him my suspicions.

The day rolled along fairly smoothly after that, right up until my second-to-last class of the day: chemistry. Because of strict regulations, the science labs were always closed until the teachers came and unlocked them. I don't know what they thought we were going to do in there, considering the room was almost empty except for several rows of white desks, a whiteboard, and a few lab benches. Most of the scientific equipment was locked in the back room.

This was my least favorite class—and not because of the subject or the teachers. It was because of the students.

Chatter filled the science lab halls. The bell had rung a few moments ago, and people were gradually floating away to their classes. A golden-brown, curly head was bobbing through the quickly dispersing crowd, heading toward us. My heart clenched in my chest, and I turned away. I didn't want to speak to Amanda Dawson. A cold animosity ran deep between us, and I didn't know why.

What had I ever done to her?

Everyone avoided Amanda and her crew, KARMA, as though they were a deadly virus. Rafe's reputation paled in comparison. Her voice was unnecessarily loud as she headed to the science lab. I gripped my books tightly, afraid she'd make an example of me in front of everyone.

I wasn't sure I had the courage to stand up for myself.

Not in front of all these people who would be watching me with hungry eyes, perhaps waiting for a bitch fight to take place. That wasn't going to happen. Not here, not now. Surely, Amanda wouldn't dare speak to me after what had happened—

"Hey, Ava. How about you move out of my way? You're kinda blocking the classroom." There was the jingle of what sounded like teacher's keys from behind me. I stumbled out of the way but glanced up once I had my back pressed against the lockers beside the lab rooms.

"Where did you get those keys?" I asked her, surprising myself.

Amanda actually looked up, her golden curls bouncing as she moved. Her eyes were the color of deep, rich wood, but after the hours she'd spent in juvenile detention with her cronies, they had developed a colder edge, making them devoid of any warmth or friendliness. Her face used to be rounded and very pretty but now looked sharper and angular, the product of all the weight she had lost.

"Where do you think, honey? I stole them," she

said, her voice like poison. I dropped my gaze to the badly carpeted floor and waited until she'd slid the key in the lock and then I dared to look back up at her. There was a click as she unlocked the door and then it swung open. The class shambled in after Amanda, but I remained outside the room for a few moments.

"We're not supposed to…" My voice weakened and trailed off at the disbelieving looks my classmates shot me.

"Be more like Kesley, Ava," said a voice from inside the classroom. Amanda. "Be *fearless* for once." Her words shot right through me, painful and tight. But the way she'd spoken was as if she'd known Kesley. I pushed down the confusion, the uncertainty, and entered the room, shutting the door quietly behind me. I made my way to my seat beside my lab partner, whose name I couldn't remember at the moment. Unbidden, my gaze found its way to Amanda. She stood at the teacher's desk, riffling through class notes. She looked up when she noticed my eyes locked on her.

A nasty grin spread across her lips, making her face look oddly grotesque. She slammed the papers back down onto the desk with a bang and spoke with a deliberately loud voice so it carried.

"Looks like we're experimenting with acids today,"

she said. The quiet talk that had filled the room dimmed as everyone watched Amanda. That was one of her many talents—she could get a whole classroom hooked on her words without even *trying*. My hand, which was lying in my lap, tightened into a fist. I let my caramel-colored hair fall over my face, hiding the left half—the half I knew everyone was going to be looking at right now.

Be fearless. Fearless, Ava. Be strong. Like Kesley.

Amanda eyed the room as if making sure people were paying attention before fixing me with a cold stare. A harsh, bright light seemed to be glaring down on me. Eyes from every corner of the room were boring into me, cutting like knives. That nasty smile twisted into a sneer as Amanda leaned against the teacher's chair, tilting her head to the side in a mock-sympathetic gesture. She said, "And I would really hate to see you on the receiving end of that again. Wouldn't you?" Her words slammed into me with the force of a truck. Acid, acid, acid. Never did I want to hear that word again…not after…

Fearless, I reminded myself. *Be fearless.*

The sharp grating sound of the chair against the floor told me I'd stood. I felt blood rush into my ears and a strange light-headed feeling propelled me forward. *Thump, thump, thump* went my heart. Again and again.

I didn't feel like Ava anymore.

I felt like a character in a movie or book, acting their part.

A ragged breathing sounded around me, magnified in the silence. Was it mine? I think so. *Fearless*, I reminded myself. *Do it. Just do it.* Before my mind could catch up to my movements, I'd rounded the edge of the teacher's desk and was face-to-face with Amanda. For the briefest, most fleeting of moments, I thought I saw a flash of uncertainty cross her features—but it vanished as quickly as it had come. My fists clenched. Heart pumped. Legs moved closer to her without my brain's permission. Part of me—the reasonable part that was no longer in control—screamed at me to get away, to stop this before things got out of hand. But it was too late. I was past the point of reasoning with myself.

Amanda took a step backward, closer to the teacher's cabinet.

My fingers grabbed hold of her collared shirt, and I shoved her back against the glass-fronted cabinets with as much force as I could muster. I hardly registered the shattering sound. Glass fell like rain to the floor, slanting over us in sharp waves. Pain contorted

Amanda's face as a piece of glass slashed her cheek, blood dripping to her chin.

She stared at me, eyes widening in shock.

Before she was able to do more than gape at me in disbelief, I drew back my fist and punched her as hard as I could. Her head snapped to the side, a grunt of pain escaping her lips. Screams and shouts were coming from my classmates, but they sounded faraway, muted, cut through by the sound of quickly approaching footsteps clicking down the hall.

Someone gripped my upper arm painfully, pulling me away from Amanda. And then: "Miss Dawson! Miss Hale! Come with me *now*, please."

My chemistry teacher led us down the carpeted halls and a few flights of stairs, her clicking heels against the linoleum floor sounding like a death march.

I rubbed my knuckles, knowing there would be bruises.

What the hell had gotten into me back there? Why had I acted like that? I was a *good girl*. I didn't pick fights. I did my homework, kept my head down. My blood still boiled from Amanda's words. I cast a sideways glance at her as we crossed the small court-yard that led to the principal's office. I noticed that her demeanor was cool and confident as she walked just behind me. I suppose a trip to the principal's office was just like going to buy a carton of milk for her.

But my own insides squirmed and twisted like they were full of worms.

I waited just outside the door to the principal's office, feeling the sharp throb in my knuckles. Amanda emerged much later, adhesive medical tape clinging to her cheek. I looked away, ashamed, and focused on the principal's door. I could hear my teacher's quiet, angry words.

Moments later, the door embossed with the golden words *Mr. Bernard* swung open and my chemistry teacher strode out without a second glance, leaving us to deal with the wrath of Mr. Bernard by ourselves. He appeared at the door, graying hair and horn-rimmed glasses and all. He didn't say a word as we stepped into the room, although he pointed at two chairs that had been set up in front of his mahogany desk.

"Sit down," he said. Amanda and I sat. Two manila folders were sitting on top of his desk—our files, I realized. It wasn't hard to see whose belonged to whom: mine was pathetically thin, while Amanda's was bursting at the seams.

Once we had taken a seat, Mr. Bernard rounded the

corner to his desk but did not sit. Instead, he looked down at us, eyes glinting with suppressed anger. I spent the next ten minutes in silence as I glared out the open window, staring at the flickers of filtering gray light and completely tuning out his lecture. I barely listened as he told us how "disappointed" he was in our actions and how he "expected better" from someone like me. He demanded to know what had happened, but both Amanda and I sat as tightly shut as clams.

"Very well. You will both receive one week's worth of detention," he said. Mr. Bernard turned his attention to me. "Miss Hale, this will add on to your previous punishment from Mrs. York. You will both start this afternoon."

And that was it. Amanda left without a word, hardly even a nod, but I needed a moment longer to gather my thoughts.

My hand was on the doorknob when Mr. Bernard spoke.

"Miss Hale?"

"Yeah?"

"Don't let what happened to Kesley change you."

My fingers tightened on the doorknob. I didn't answer, but all I could think was: *I think it already has.*

I didn't go to last period.

Since I was already in deep shit, I figured it wouldn't really matter if I ditched one more class. There was no point leaving the school premises, considering I'd have to be back there for detention, so I hung out in the girls' bathroom.

A long mirror stretched from one side to the other, chipped yellow-brown tiles decorating the very undesirable room. Rows of sinks with faucets sat below the mirror. I stood in the center of the room, closing my eyes. But then I yanked them open, forcing them to look at the girl in the reflection. She looked no different than the girl yesterday or even the day before that, but somehow there was a hardened edge to her eyes that hadn't been there a couple months back.

And sometimes, looking in the mirror, I didn't even recognize myself.

Sometimes, looking at myself—flat, brown-blond hair, brown eyes, and the pink, rough scars that ran from the tip of my forehead to the base of my collarbone, stretching along my neck—I didn't feel real. I felt fragmented.

I touched the scar along my face, feeling the bumps and ridges, reminding me it was *real*. That *I* was real.

I couldn't remember much of what happened the night of the accident. The doctors told me the memory loss was because of posttraumatic stress, but I *did* remember brief feelings and thoughts. Sometimes, I would wake late at night, my throat clogged with a scream, the scent of burning flesh in my nose. Other times, something would trigger a memory: I'd look at a linoleum floor at a certain angle and remember clearly the feel of it against my knees as I fell after the acid hit. Or I'd hear a voice in a crowd that brought back fleeting memories of the police who questioned me.

Once, a glass beaker had smashed in science class, and the memory of the acid bottle shattering had been just as sharp.

Yet they were only snatches, hints at a past locked away. If I thought about it, I didn't really *want* to know the whole, unedited truth.

The screech of a bathroom stall door made me flinch back to the present.

I sighed, pulled my hair over my face once more to cover the scar, and turned to leave. The scar didn't hurt anymore, but people always stared.

And with recent events, people had been looking at
me a lot.

I walked out of afternoon detention feeling somewhat relieved.

Amanda, predictably, hadn't shown, and it was nice
knowing I wouldn't have to put up with her death glare
burning a hole in the back of my head. But underneath
the relief, my nerves jangled, knowing my mother
would've heard what happened at school today.

Instead of texting Lia to pick me up, I was going
to walk home, despite the misty rain beginning to
fall. Like the coward I was, I knew that would delay
the moment when I would actually have to face my
mother. She worked as a chemist in a lab just outside of
town, and today was her day off. I never knew exactly
what she did. She was always sketchy on the details. All
I knew was that it involved acids and chemicals and all
sorts of things I'd rather be ignorant about.

I paused at the school entrance when I spotted a tall
figure leaning against the school's ivy-wrapped gate. I'd
been avoiding Rafe all day, but my luck seemed to have
run dry. A cold shiver danced down my spine, and I

glanced to my left and then my right. I couldn't see any way of walking past without him noticing me. A nervous thrill went through me at the idea of confronting him.

"Rafe?" I said softly as I drew nearer. He turned at the sound of my voice, his hair dripping with rainwater, making his dark-brown hair look black. He shot me a crooked smile, eyes twinkling a bit. There wasn't a hint of guilt on his face. Did that mean he hadn't done what I thought he'd done or that he was incapable of feeling guilty? I thought back to what Lia had told me in the car the other day. How well did I know Rafe, *really*?

Before he left...before the funeral, I'd thought I knew him well.

He was intelligent, with confidence that bordered on arrogance, but I couldn't deny the violent streak that had sent him to juvenile detention.

I had no idea what he was capable of. On one hand, he was the caring boy I had grown up with. The one who I'd climbed trees with and eaten candy with until we felt ill. The one who Kesley and I would walk the streets with until night fell, then stay out late to count the stars. But he had changed subtly over the years since his parents' divorce, growing more antagonistic until we'd drifted slowly apart.

"I wasn't sure whether you had a ride or not," Rafe told me as I stopped in front of him. My eyes slid beyond the school gates, and I saw a black car parked a few yards away from where we were standing. Illegally parked, of course. The law was beneath Rafe. Always had been. I swallowed nervously, rocking back on my heels.

"If I wanted a ride, I'd call my boyfriend," I pointed out coldly.

A grin. "And yet he's nowhere in sight."

I fiddled with the strap of my bag and decided to come clean. "I don't exactly want to go home, not just yet."

A strange expression flickered over Rafe's face. "Because of Amanda?"

"You know about that?"

He flicked a brow at me. "Come Monday, the whole school will know about that." It took all my self-restraint not to groan out loud. Why the hell had I done it? Couldn't I have just sat down quietly and said and done nothing? But the anger that had coursed through me at her words was like nothing I'd ever felt before.

"Yes, because of Amanda. I hate disappointing my mom, you know? And with everything that's been going on lately…" I bit down on my lip until it hurt.

Rafe squinted up at the sky. The rain was coming down thicker now, pelting us more ferociously. "I don't know about you, but I don't want to get drenched." He started walking toward his car. He paused when he saw I wasn't following. "Coming?"

I weighed my options.

On the one hand, I was not convinced of his innocence, despite how guilt-free he might appear. But on the other—how many opportunities like this was I going to get to question him? Curiosity won out over fear. So I followed his example and walked to the curb.

I slid into the warm leather seat and shut the door.

"Of all the people you could choose to assault," Rafe murmured, "it had to be the toughest girl in school." And then: "Well, the second-toughest girl in the school."

"Who's first?"

"Kesley was first," he said.

"Oh." I said nothing more, leaving an awkward silence. That was the key word, wasn't it? *Was.* The engine hummed in the background. Rain pelted against the glass, but Rafe flicked the wipers on, and the squeak of the blades was added to the din. Heat blasted from the vents, though it was very welcome. It washed away the cold that clung to me.

Rafe turned to me, gesturing at something. "Mind if I…?"

I glanced at the cigarettes, then looked away. "Fine. Whatever."

He laughed.

"What?" I said rather defensively.

"You sound a lot like Kesley," was his only response, but he still reached for the pack and lit one, flicking the ash out the partially open window. He looked at me for a moment, rolling the cigarette between his fingers while smoke curled out the window. I watched the rain consume the smoke, wondering *how* to ask what I wanted to ask.

A ghost of a smile crossed his face. "And that *looks* a lot like Kesley."

I just squinted at him in confusion.

"Whenever Kesley wanted to ask me something, a favor—to do her homework usually—her brows would narrow, and she'd squint."

"Oh." My stomach fluttered with nerves. The words hovered on my lips, but I couldn't seem to push them out of my mouth.

"Go on," he said gently.

I sucked in a breath. My heart steadied a little, which was the most I was going to get. The words fell out of my mouth in a heap. "Did you kill my sister?"

An awfully loud silence filled the car. The purr of the engine and squeak of the wipers were magnified tenfold. The slam of a car door sounded from somewhere, but neither of us looked up to see where it came from. *Plop, plop.* The rain continued, louder than before.

"Well," said Rafe dryly, "aren't you bold?"

I bristled at the edge of amusement to his voice. Heat flared into my cheeks. All of a sudden, everything was too hot, and I was grateful Rafe had left the window open.

I stared at my knotted hands in my lap.

"I saw—"

"—a plane ticket," Rafe finished.

"You knew," I said, lifting my gaze to his face. "Why didn't you say anything?"

Rafe shot me an indescribable look. Frustration? "You ran out of the café before I'd even paid," he said. "You didn't exactly give me a chance."

"I'm giving you a chance now," I said quietly, not moving my eyes from my hands.

Rafe took another drag from the cigarette before answering. "You're right," he finally said. "I *didn't* come back after she was killed. But also I didn't get to see her before she died."

"What's that supposed to mean?"

"Three days before Kesley died, she called me in Vancouver." His jaw clenched. "God, Ava, she sounded *scared*. She wasn't making much sense either. She only told me that something strange was happening—and that she needed to speak to me. I managed to convince my father to let me come back here early to get ready for the school semester." Since his parents' divorce, he'd split his time between his mother in Circling Pines and his father in Vancouver.

"Did she tell you...?" My voice broke. Clearing my throat, I continued, "Did she tell you what was wrong?"

Rafe just shook his head. "No. She didn't."

But I still couldn't help noticing he wouldn't quite meet my eyes. Besides, if he'd really come back to Circling Pines the day the ticket indicated, why wouldn't he have had enough time to see Kesley?

Again, the feeling he wasn't being entirely honest with me made my stomach curl with anxiety.

"I need you to say it, Rafe." I hated myself for how

weak, how desperate, I sounded. Silence. For a long, long, long moment, there was nothing but silence.

And then: "I didn't murder Kesley. I never would have hurt her. *Never*."

I deflated. All the tension, the fear inside me leaked away, replaced with cold numbness. It didn't last long.

"Do you think she knew she was going to die?" I couldn't help but ask. The thought made me shiver in horror, and my toes curled. I blinked and wasn't all that surprised to feel the wetness of tears in my eyes.

Rafe answered honestly. "I don't know. But she knew something."

I looked out the window at the rain washing down the drains and at the sky laden with clouds. The street was empty, but I no longer felt safe. A streak of lightning split the sky, followed by the sharp snapping of thunder.

I was suddenly glad I hadn't walked home by myself.

Another question rose to the surface of my mind. "Did you love her? Kesley, I mean."

"Yes," Rafe whispered very softly. "I loved her like a sister."

"Just as a sister?" I couldn't keep the sharp edge of accusation from entering my voice. I glanced over at him just in time to see a smile quirk his mouth.

"Would that make you jealous, Ava?"

"That's not what I meant," I said, feeling warmth spread across my neck. "I just…wondered. She adored you, you know."

The smile slipped from his mouth. "I know. But… no, I never thought of her in that way."

"Why not?" I asked.

"Because it would be pretty gross to date your own sister."

"You know what I mean," I snapped.

From the corner of my eye, I saw him shrug. "That doesn't matter, does it? She felt like a sister to me, so that's what she was, relation or not."

I turned my gaze to the rain-washed windows.

I don't know whether I believed him—my head was already spinning with too many thoughts I'd have to untangle later. There was one thing I did know though: the fear I'd felt when I'd seen Rafe standing at the gate had dissolved.

Maybe I shouldn't have believed his story so easily.

Maybe I should have asked him more questions.

Maybe he would be my downfall too.

I'd almost forgotten about the whole incident with Amanda by the time I got home, but reality slammed into me when I heard the *click-click* of my mother's heels. I repressed a grimace. What was I supposed to *say* to her? My mother had a phone clutched in her hands when I walked through the high, arched doors. I only needed to take one look at her to see the fury— and disappointment—written over her face.

I closed my eyes briefly, waiting for the tirade to come. And come it did.

"I just got off the phone with Mr. Bernard," she said, sounding like she was speaking through a clenched jaw. Her voice was as cold as ice—or at least as cold as the rain pelting down outside. "And he so *kindly* informed me that you were given an extra week of detention for assaulting Miss Dawson. You are *so* lucky she doesn't want to press charges." She sounded as if *she* wanted to press charges on behalf of Amanda. Guilt twisted in my chest.

I said nothing for a moment. Only stared at my feet.

"I don't really want to talk about it, okay? I haven't had a great day."

"Well, that's too bad. We *have* to talk about it."

My eyes flashed up to meet hers, my gaze just as steely. "What do you want me to say exactly? That

Amanda Dawson absolutely hates me, and I have no idea why? That I finally snapped because I don't want to have to put up with her shit anymore?"

"*Ava!* Watch your language—"

My voice rose. "And oh yeah, maybe, just maybe, because my sister's killer is still on the loose?"

My mother's mouth softened, just slightly. "So this is about Kesley."

Wasn't everything?

"No," I whispered. My voice didn't sound convincing in the slightest.

"Then *why*, sweetie? Tell me, and I can help—"

"No, you can't," I said flatly.

My mother's jaw tightened, but she knew she wasn't going to win this fight. "We'll talk later then," she said, even though I knew we wouldn't. "Go have a hot shower, okay? You look like you're freezing."

Because of our parents' fates, our early childhoods were riddled with darkness, but despite that, there are memories I hold on to dearly. Many of them include you.

If I had known they were finite, I think I would have guarded them more closely. Cataloged them. Made sure I remembered every small, insignificant moment, wrapped them up tightly. There were the times you and I skipped first period to have coffee. Or the time you lay, arms outstretched, in the middle of the road. I shrieked at you to move— what if someone hit you?—but you just laughed like it was no big deal.

Fearless.

That was the word that came to mind when you did crazy, incomprehensible things.

So now, for me, memories are as precious as gold.

Memories like the ones we shared every summer: after the school year finished, we'd pack our bags, shove them in the back of Mom's SUV, and make the trip to Yoho National Park. Our favorite place to go camping was Lake O'Hara. Remember that time when we sat around the fire while we roasted marshmallows? You said you loved that place because of the calm, peaceful lake, the way the breeze whispered in the trees, the way we could count the stars in the sky.

You told me the lake was beautiful beyond measure.

And if you'd told me that night, Kesley, that something as awful as your death would happen in a place so beautiful, I wouldn't have believed you. Because who would have guessed the place you loved so much would be your downfall...

Five

THE WEEKEND STRETCHED OUT BEFORE me, empty, and I worried what that emptiness would bring. Memories, I knew. Ones I'd sooner forget. Because memories, I was beginning to understand, left deeper scars than physical wounds.

As much as I wanted to stay curled under the warm blankets all morning, I realized that was just going to make me feel worse, so I crept down the stairs and into the kitchen. My mother was flicking through the pages of the morning newspaper, a cup of coffee beside her.

She glanced up when I entered. "Want some coffee?"

"Sure," I said and slid into the seat opposite her. She poured me a steaming cup, and I curved my hands around the warm edges but did not drink.

"Is there something wrong? You're not usually up this early," she pointed out. I sighed.

"Nothing's wrong," I assured her, tracing the edge of the cup with a finger. "I just wanted to know if you've been to the police station lately."

My mother pushed her cup of coffee away as if it suddenly revolted her. She didn't look at me, but something sad passed over her face. When she'd signed the contracts to become our legal parent, she hadn't counted on one of her foster daughters being murdered.

Kesley and I had been her legal foster daughters since I was six years old. She is, and always would be, the closest thing I had to a living mother.

"As soon as I know something about Kesley," she said, "you'll know too."

"Oh."

Mom said nothing more on the subject. I picked up a napkin and shredded it, not looking at her.

I was being unfair to expect so much from the police. Right? Homicide cases were few around here, so I doubted our small-town police force had much experience with them. But still—there had been *nothing* new on the case since Kesley's body had been discovered.

"Kesley needs *justice*," I said, my voice sharp with frustration.

"Ava..." My mother's voice broke. She placed her hand on mine. "I know it's hard. But we just have to sit tight, okay? The police *will* find out who did this to Kesley. I promise you."

But that's the thing about promises, isn't it? They can't always be kept.

No matter how good the intentions behind them are.

My mother continued speaking, but I wasn't really paying attention at that point. She sighed and slid her chair back. "It's getting late," she told me, "and I have some errands to run. Have any plans for today?"

"No," I said.

"Well." She pulled her bag over her shoulder and headed toward the front door. "If you do decide to do something, just be careful, okay?"

"Careful?"

"I don't know how safe it is out there anymore, Ava," was all she said.

A few moments later, the slam of the door told me she had left. There was a crunch of gravel as she backed out of the driveway, and that was it. Silence. Sweet, terrifying silence. Soon, the memories would come. And then the despair.

And then—

The doorbell rang. I scraped my chair back and went to get the door. Jackson was waiting outside, and he must've seen my expression. "What's wrong?" he asked.

"Still nothing new about Kesley," I whispered.

I sank into his arms, pressing my face into his chest. Everything felt better when he was with me. Not good but bearable.

He pulled back a little to look at me, and sympathy softened his features. "Everything will be fine," he said so sincerely that I almost believed it. "I know it will. You'll have your justice." Another promise, another good intention. My gaze flicked over his pale-green eyes, brown hair, and the slight scruff on his chin.

"I'm not sure that's possible anymore," I said. "It's been two months, Jackson. What if they *never* find out who did this to her? What if it remains unsolved? I don't know how I can live with that—"

He cupped my face and pressed a kiss to my lips, cutting off the rest of my words. "You'll get closure," he promised me.

"I don't think I want closure anymore," I whispered. "I just want my sister back."

He had no reply to that.

The rest of the day passed quickly now that Jackson was here. He'd brought me flowers too: white lilies that now sit on my bedside table. I wondered if he knew white lilies were symbolic of death. We said nothing more about Kesley and focused instead on school, until he saw the photo by my bed.

"Hey," Jackson said, breaking through my thoughts of algebraic formulas. "Where was this taken?"

Light spilled onto the photo he was looking at. Sitting on my nightstand was a picture framed with ornate diamond-like jewels.

The light gleaming off them was almost blinding.

The picture had been taken this summer—the last summer Kesley would ever have. She had an arm slung around me, and we both were smiling. In the background was a gleaming lake surrounded by trees. It was obviously windy because our hair trailed out behind us, and Kesley was pulling long blond ribbons of hair from her eyes, throwing the image slightly off-balance. I liked how this picture wasn't entirely perfect.

A curling blue ribbon was in Kesley's hand.

The words were stuck in my throat. I had to take

several deep breaths before answering. "Lake O'Hara," I said. *Where she was murdered*, I didn't add.

"Oh." He fell silent. He sat up, running a hand through his hair, his face twisting slightly, deep in thought. "Do you think...?"

"What?" I said quickly.

"Doesn't matter," he muttered and looked out the window.

"Do I think that whoever killed my sister knew we went there every summer?" I asked for him.

"Well, yeah."

"I guess so," I said, "but everyone knew that. It could be anyone in this town." Going to Lake O'Hara had become a family tradition, so it was no secret where we went every year. It hardly narrowed down the list of suspects.

But as I thought about it, it *was* just too much of a coincidence that my sister's killer had chosen that place in particular.

My mind flickered back to my last conversation with Rafe. Could Kesley have realized that someone was after her? Had she even known she was going to *die*? And if that was the case...then why the silence? The secrecy?

I felt like the answers were just out of my reach.

My face must've shown that, because at that moment, Jackson shifted our books and came to sit beside me. I tried to rearrange my expression into something blank, but I don't think it worked very well.

When Jackson spoke, his lips were at my ear.

"Try to think about something else for a while," he said. I pressed myself closer into his embrace, letting his arms settle around my waist.

"Like what?" I said with a smile.

"Like this." And suddenly his lips were at my neck, sparking hot trails where his mouth touched. Something inside me shattered, and I let go. I pulled him close, curling my hands around his collar, and wrapped my legs around his waist. At first, his lips were gentle, but as I sighed into his mouth and slipped my hands into his hair, I felt his arms tighten around me. His warm hands caressed my face—each touch leaving an icy heat behind. He leaned back—just a little—to speak. His hand still rested on my cheek.

"Better now?" he asked, slightly breathless.

"Yeah," I agreed. "Better."

He pressed a tender kiss to the right side of my face. Always the right. Never the left, the scarred side.

That bothered me more than I let on.

CHAPTER
Six

I WOKE ON MONDAY WITH MY STOMACH IN a bundle of nerves.

It took me a whole two minutes of staring at the sunlight-striped ceiling before I remembered why. Amanda would be waiting for me today—and she'd want revenge. She wasn't the sort to forgive and forget, and after what I'd done to her… I considered pleading illness, but my mother would see straight through that in a heartbeat. Besides, what was the point of running from things?

It'd all catch up with me eventually.

I showered, dressed in a pale, high-collared dress with tights, and hesitated at the mirror. I was not a brazen person. I hid behind a curtain of hair and avoided eye contact with people who passed me. But today? Today was different. *I* was different. Braver somehow. Instead of letting my hair fall over my scars, I tied it into a ponytail.

I paused before leaving my room, snagging one of the blue ribbons I rarely used in my hair. This was the start of a new Ava.

A strong, fearless one.

"Strong" and "fearless" weren't words that came to mind when I thought of myself. What was so different about today? I looked into the mirror—*really* looked— but only saw the same girl I saw every other day.

"You're up early again," said Mom as I entered the kitchen. She had an apple in one hand, a phone in the other, and hadn't even looked up when I came in. She was scribbling something on a piece of paper, brows narrowed in concentration.

"No," I said, glancing at the clock. "You're just late."

"Oh yes. Dammit," she added, glowering at the paper on the table.

"What's that?" I asked, moving closer.

"Kesley's old piano tutors called… They said they

found some things of Kesley's in the practice room. You know," she added, looking at me, "old music sheets and small things like that. I thought you'd want them."

I did. I wanted them more than anything.

Fighting to keep my voice even, I asked, "Can I have the address?"

My mother hesitated. "Ava, I'm not sure that's a good idea."

"Why?" I shot back, feeling those treacherous tears sting my eyes. Did she think I couldn't handle it? "They're just *things*," I said, slightly calmer now. "I-I just think it would be nice to have them."

My mother breathed out a sigh, but eventually, she relented. "Fine. Just promise me you won't be late for school."

I rolled my eyes and took the address off the table. "I won't."

She seemed to look at me properly for the first time since I entered the room, and she said, "You've done something different with your hair."

I paused. "Yeah. I thought I'd try something different for once."

"I like it," my mother said softly. Tears shone in her eyes. "You look like Kesley."

———

The music shop was cold, dusty, and shrouded in darkness. A slice of sunlight fought its way through the filth-covered windows, but apart from that, it seemed to be a rather undesirable place to take lessons. I was ushered through the rows of overpriced gleaming instruments to the practice rooms by one of the shop assistants who barely looked at me. She unlocked the door to the one Kesley used and left me there. I stared into the unlit room for a few moments before I reached for the light switch and flicked it on.

A bag lay on the closed piano with the name Kesley stitched across the front. Music sheets spilled out, the yellow-orange of the dim light highlighting the dust. I stood there, paralyzed, for a few moments.

Perhaps my mother had been right.

Perhaps I was not ready for this.

Tears burned in my eyes. I did not let them fall. It seemed strange that something as small as a few personal items had such an effect on me. Maybe because these *meant* something. I reached into the bag without realizing it, letting my hands run through the sheets of paper. Their titles jumped out at me:

"Moonlight Sonata, Movement One," "Für Elise," "Marche Funèbre." Their titles brought back a swell of memories, of sounds that used to fill our house. I swiped at the tears falling from my eyes and dug deeper into the bag. There were a few other things—like an empty perfume bottle. When I held it close to my nose, it still smelled of jasmine. Of sorrow.

More tears prickled my eyes. I ignored them.

And there, right at the bottom of the bag, was a notebook. It was designed like a piano: white, with black keys stretching the length of the book. A pang of something shot through me, but I flipped the notebook open, teeth gritted. It felt somehow...*wrong*, morbid, to be going through a dead girl's things. Most of it, I was disappointed to find, was blank, but as I flipped to the center, a flash of color caught my eye. A phone number. I stared at it for a moment—but it didn't look familiar.

I fumbled for my phone and dialed the number.

My hands were shaking so badly that I needed three tries to get it right.

The number rang. And rang. Just when I thought nobody was going to pick up... "Cam's self-defense lessons. How may I help you?"

Self-defense? I hit End Call and sank to my knees.

Never once had I heard Kesley express an interest in self-defense. So why did she have a number for it written down in her notebook? Something Rafe had said crossed my mind.

"God, Ava, she sounded scared. She wasn't making much sense either. She only told me something strange was happening and that she needed to speak to me." Only a few days later, her body washed up on the banks of Lake O'Hara, rope wrapped around her throat like some sort of macabre necklace.

So what was the normal, logical thing for someone to do if they thought they were in danger? Learn how to defend themselves.

Little good it had done.

A doorbell tinkled from somewhere in the shop, and I flinched. Then shoving everything back into the bag, music sheets and all, I swung it over my shoulder and left the music store. The ice-cold air outside was almost welcome. It bit angrily at my face, and a vicious wind tore at my hair.

I wasn't upset anymore; I was angry.

Livid.

I couldn't help but feel...betrayed. Kesley had *known* something, something important. And she hadn't told a soul.

I walked to school in a haze, hardly noticing as the streets of Circling Pines swept by. I hadn't even realized I'd reached the school gates until I walked right into someone. "Sorry," I said without looking up.

"Oh, hey—Ava?"

My head jerked up so fast that it cracked. It was May—Jackson's older sister. They looked remarkably similar, both favoring the gentle green eyes of their mother and the sharp features of their father. Her hair, the same shade as Jackson's, brushed against her shoulders and softened her angular chin. She cocked her head to the side, rather like a bird.

She pulled out her earphones, curling them around her phone, and grinned at me. "Look. I just wanted you to know that you pulled a brilliant stunt on Friday. Seriously. I don't think anyone's stood up to Amanda like that since Kesley." Her grin, if possible, became even brighter.

I offered May a tentative smile. Out of Amanda's group, May was the only one who'd shown me the barest semblance of compassion.

"But she hates me, right?"

May just grinned wider. "Oh yeah, she does. That's the best part. I mean, it's not hard to get Amanda angry about something, but she doesn't expect it to come from someone like you." *Someone like you. Right.*

My brief flicker of irritation was whipped away when a girl with store-bought auburn hair stepped out of the crowd. Her mouth was carved into a permanent scowl, and she would have been pretty—beautiful even—if she smiled more often. Her eyes, while stunningly amber, were marred by a frosty edge that somehow took their beauty away. They swept over me with a dismissive glance. "Come on," Amanda said to May as if I weren't there, "you've wasted enough time with her."

May threw an apologetic glance over her shoulder as she walked away.

It almost made me feel bad for her.

Riley, the cropped-haired girl, turned back to me. Her body was tense, as if she were poised for a fight. "You know what they say," she said, her voice low and dangerous. "What goes around comes around."

Karma. The word flashed through my mind unbidden.

May and Riley vanished into the crowd, leaving me with an ice-cold feeling that embedded itself in my bones. Perhaps May was okay with what I'd done to Amanda—but Riley was another story altogether.

"Just ignore them," said a voice from behind me.

"They're *all* talk and no action." I turned to see Lia standing there. Her hand was clenched around the handle of a leather handbag, her skin paling. Her gaze was focused on the swelling crowd and just as cold. Lia liked Amanda's group about as much as I did. A small smile twitched onto my face, though it was humorless.

"I'm not so sure about that," I murmured. "Riley seemed pretty sincere about getting back at me."

Lia lifted her shoulders in an elegant shrug. "Whatever," she said, flipping her hair over her shoulder. "They'd have to get through me first anyway." She glanced at me, some of the frozenness in her eyes melting as she regarded me. I smiled—a *real* smile—as she looped her arm around mine and pulled me farther onto the school grounds. People milled around us. A few of them glanced up at me as we passed, but no remarks came my way for once.

"Everyone's heard about it, of course," Lia continued as we wove through the crowds.

I sighed in dismay. "Great. That's *exactly* what I want."

Lia laughed. "That's the spirit, eh? At least you got a good punch in."

Thankfully, Lia said nothing more on the subject and instead started talking about this season's fashion—but

I wasn't paying attention. Over her shoulder, I could see Rafe leaning against his locker, eyes fixed on the two of us. Heat flushed my cheeks. Sure, I was used to attention—the looks, those awful pitying looks— but there was no pity in those blue eyes. There was an intense, calculating edge to his expression, something I wasn't entirely comfortable with.

Still, I didn't look away.

Girls were admiring him from all angles, attracted to him like bees to a flower, but Rafe paid them no attention. Unusual for him, to say the least.

Lia didn't take long to notice that my attention was focused somewhere else, and she twisted around to see what had caught my gaze. Rafe half smiled, half smirked when he caught both of us looking and walked away.

I'd stopped walking now. People pushed past us, but neither Lia nor I moved. I felt my cheeks warm with color. Why had I been caught looking at another boy—least of all Rafe—while I had a boyfriend?

I heard Lia groan from beside me. "You haven't been hanging around with him, have you?" She really didn't have to ask me that; I heard the answer in the disapproving pitch of her voice. So I just shrugged and looked away.

"He's nicer than you think." Why was I defending him?

I wasn't looking at her, but I could clearly imagine her rolling her eyes. "Fine. Whatever. Did you see the way he was looking at you? It was creepy, like he knew something you didn't."

Yes, there was. I just didn't know what yet.

"Anyway," Lia said, pulling me deeper into the crowd. "Want to go for coffee after school?"

"Sure."

"Jackson coming?"

I cast her a sidelong look, wondering why that mattered. "Yeah, sure. I'll ask."

———

Rafe was sitting on my bed when I got home. And if that weren't creepy enough, he'd drawn the blinds, shadowing everything in semidarkness. A dusty, yellowed guitar rested in his arms, its strap frayed, worn from love. Watching him there, holding *that* guitar, made my heart ache.

"If Kesley were still alive," I said, "she'd kill you for touching that."

A flicker of *something* passed over Rafe's features,

followed moments later by a crooked smile. "You're probably right," he said.

I let my bag fall to the ground. "Rafe, what are you doing here?"

His smile didn't slip at the sudden coldness in my tone. He glanced up briefly. "Hi to you too," he said, plucking at the guitar strings. He played a familiar melody I couldn't quite place.

Indignation flared. I said, "What are you doing here? And how the hell did you get inside?"

Rafe flicked a finger up, a gleaming silver key ring hanging there. "Kesley told me where the key was," he said. "Under the mat."

I made a mental note to hide the spare key somewhere else.

"So," said Rafe, "I see you're still in one piece."

I breathed out a sigh. "Yeah, for now anyway. Riley was giving me the death glare this morning." I sat down on the bed beside him, legs crossed and acutely aware of the close distance between us. I couldn't look at him, so I just stared at my pale hands. "Was there something you wanted from me, Rafe?"

"What?"

"You broke into my house for a reason," I said dryly.

His shoulders lifted into a shrug. "I had the key. So

technically, I wasn't *breaking in.*" Then he looked at me and said, "I wanted to see you. I wanted to make sure you were all right."

I felt my mouth twist. "What, one sister's gone, so you're moving on to the other?" Rafe stopped plucking the melody to angle a look in my direction. Shame prickled through me at the thought of what I'd just said. I stared down again at my fingers, which I had been knotting together subconsciously.

"You're upset," he said gently. "But that's not what I'm doing here."

"I'm sorry." I wished I hadn't pulled my hair up this morning. Now I didn't have anything to hide behind. I was exposed, vulnerable.

Rafe touched a strand of blond brown hair that had fallen across my face.

"I like your hair like that," he murmured. "It makes you look more like Kesley." *More like Kesley.* I looked away.

"Am I just another Kesley to you?"

Rafe straightened, his brows pulling together. "That's not what I meant. Not at all. You just seem… different. Stronger. More like how I remember you when we were kids."

A thrill shot through me.

"Thanks, I guess." I fiddled with the hem of my dress, then stood up.

I dragged my backpack over to my study desk and began to pull out books, piling them neatly into stacks. "As you can see," I said, unnerved that he could be so *comfortable* right now, sitting on my bed and plucking on the guitar, "Amanda hasn't gotten to me. Yet. So you can leave." I moved over to yank open the blinds, and afternoon sunlight spilled through the windows.

Silence for a moment. And then, "You didn't go to Kesley's grave today."

It wasn't a question, but I replied anyway. "No, I didn't." I paused for a moment, then asked, "Rafe, how did you know I do that?" Had he been following me too? Like Jackson? Though I suspected my mother had asked Jackson to keep an eye on me.

Rafe looked at me. His eyes, sharp and calculating, were narrowed slightly. "You're not the only one who visits Kesley's grave," he said. He didn't elaborate, but I didn't need him to. I silently lowered myself onto the bed beside him again, and we let our grief wrap itself around us. Gray and heavy.

The melancholy guitar notes filled the room, and I listened for a few minutes. "I never knew you played the guitar," I said softly, as if I were unwilling to break the paper-thin atmosphere the music had created.

I wasn't looking at him, but I heard the grin in his voice. "There are many things you don't know about me, Ava. Music just happens to be one of them." He shot a sideways glance at me. "I could teach you if you wanted."

"Okay then, man of many talents. What else don't I know about you?"

A flicker of surprise creased his forehead, but it vanished so quickly that I could have imagined it. His face had smoothed back into a blank mask; the moment had already passed. "What do you want to know?" His voice was guarded.

"What exactly did Kesley tell you the night before you came back?" I stared at him, my gaze unflinching.

Rafe ran a hand through his hair, frustrated. "I was talking about myself. Not Kesley."

"You're avoiding the question."

"I've already told you. She never told me what was going on. She said she needed me to come back to Circling Pines and that the situation had changed. I don't...I don't know anything else."

"But you came back to Circling Pines after she died, right?"

"Yes."

"Kesley died over a month ago. So what have you been doing all this time? And what did she mean when she said the situation had changed?"

Rafe shrugged. "I worked at the gas station near the highway for a while. Caught up with schoolwork. Enrolled back in high school. And if I knew more about what Kesley said, so would you." He answered my questions with ease, but he wouldn't look me in the eye.

What was that supposed to mean? That he was hiding something?

"I don't know why you're lying to me, Rafe," I said flatly.

"I'm not lying to you."

"Yeah, maybe, but you're not telling me everything, are you?"

He couldn't answer my question in good conscience without lying outright, so he said nothing. I said, "You said she was scared when she called you. Not long after, she was killed." I turned to him, not caring about the tears that shone in my eyes. "I think she *knew* someone was after her."

Rafe closed his eyes briefly. When he opened them, they were glistening.

"That's the logical explanation, isn't it?" he said.

And the most horrible. What was so awful that it had stopped her from telling someone, anyone, her fears?

I stared absently out the window. A single star-shaped leaf floated through the air, joining its fellows on the carpet of orange and brown that stretched the length of the street. I felt a little like that. Withered and tired. The light was fading quickly, streaking the sky with dirty ribbons of deep orange and yellow.

A crunch of wheels on gravel brought my attention to the driveway. My heart lurched, and I shot Rafe a panicked look.

"You should go," I whispered. "My mother's back."

"No, I should speak to her."

"*What?* Rafe, no, that's really not necessary—" But he'd already leaped from the bed. He glanced in the vanity mirror that hung on my wall and, after attempting to neaten his hair, headed to the door.

"This is a bad idea," I warned. "And what does it matter what your hair looks like?"

He glanced over his shoulder with a grin. "It's always nice to make a good first impression on parents," he said.

I blinked. "You're not my boyfriend."

"No, not yet. But the last time I saw your mother was before I left for Vancouver." *No, not yet?* What was *that* supposed to mean? A curious combination of anger and embarrassment burned inside me. I ducked my head, knowing I was blushing. There wasn't time to question him further. The slam of the car door echoed down the driveway, and we both left my room.

I'd just poured Rafe a cup of orange juice when the front door opened.

Anxiety made my fingers slip on the glass I handed Rafe. It clattered to the table, but Rafe steadied it by curving his hand over mine. I pulled away more quickly than was probably polite.

What would my mother think of Rafe now? Would she, like me, immediately think the worst of him? But then I wondered: why did I care what my mother thought?

"Sorry I'm late, sweetie," I heard my mother call from the hallway. "Traffic was awful. They're doing more construction on the highway, and it slowed down... Oh." She stepped into the kitchen, eyes falling on Rafe.

"Hi, Mom," I said rather weakly. What little courage I still had left seemed to drain out of me when I saw the way she was looking at Rafe. Not...hostile exactly. But definitely *not* friendly either.

Rafe stood. "Hi, Mrs. Kingston."

My mother dropped her bag on the counter and said, "You know to call me Diana. You've come back from Vancouver then?"

"Yeah. A few days ago."

"You missed your best friend's funeral."

I was somewhat taken aback by the chilled edge to her voice and the bluntness. "*Mom*," I hissed. She didn't even spare me a glance.

Rafe lifted an eyebrow but didn't say anything, which was smart. If he said the wrong thing around her, especially concerning Kesley, things would not be pretty.

"Sorry," she said, but it didn't sound much like an apology.

Rafe shot a glance at me and half smiled at my mother. "I'll see you at school, yeah?" he said to me. I nodded and watched him leave the kitchen. A moment later, the quiet *click* of the door told me he'd left.

I turned to my mother, eyes narrowed. "That was uncalled for," I said.

Diana didn't answer me straight away. Instead, she moved to the fridge, started pulling out vegetables, and reached for a knife on the counter. The blade caught a stream of light coming in from the window, reflecting brilliant, white light.

A blade raised high. Light pouring from the window. A voice: frail, unsure, broken, saying, "Ava. Go. Please, just go!" And then...blackness.

The sound of the knife slamming down on a carrot brought me back.

"I just can't believe the audacity of that boy. Kesley dies. He doesn't even bother coming to her funeral—and now he thinks he can just waltz back into your life? Can't he see you're *hurting*?"

I stared at her blankly. What was she even talking about? I didn't remember. I watched the knife slice tip first into another carrot. I waited for it to trigger another...*something*, but the moment never came.

I closed my eyes briefly. The light on the knife reminded me of a recurring nightmare I'd had as a child. In it, I was standing outside a long, dark room with one window, light streaming through, and a knife lying on the counter. I could never pinpoint *what* about the dream terrified me so much, because I would wake before I stepped into the room. I remembered telling the dream to a psychologist I'd had as a child. She'd crossed her legs and said, "It was a dream, Ava. Nothing in a dream can hurt you."

My rapidly beating heart began to slow, enough for me to pull myself back to the present.

My mother had stopped chopping. "Ava? Are you listening?"

Oh, right. "Yeah."

"Was he in your room?" she asked suddenly.

I felt my cheeks flame. The best option here, I thought, was to lie. "*No!* No, of course he wasn't. Why would you think that? And besides, you know I have a boyfriend."

"Good," she said. "Jackson's a nice kid."

"As opposed to Rafe?"

"Yes, as opposed to Rafe."

I tucked a stray lock of hair behind my ears, feeling uncomfortable. "That's not fair, Mom. He was one of Kesley's closest friends. And mine too."

My mother spun around, the knife still clutched in her hands. I flinched. "For God's *sake*, Ava! You *know* what happened. He went completely off the rails when his parents divorced! He beat up his social worker and got sent to juvenile *detention*. You don't need him hurting you too."

"He's *always* been there for Kesley and me," I whispered.

"Well, she's dead, isn't she? Clearly, he wasn't there enough for her."

I tried to swallow, but my mouth was dry. "Are

you saying you think Rafe was somehow involved with Kesley's…"

"No." My mother breathed out a sigh. "I don't know, Ava. Maybe. All I know for sure is that I've been your legal guardian for only ten years, and I've already lost one of my daughters. I can't lose you too."

I felt tears burn my eyes. I don't think I'd ever heard her talk like that, with such raw honesty in her voice.

There was no point in pushing the conversation about Rafe further. It would only upset her. So I turned and made my way back to my room, eyes falling on the guitar Rafe had left sitting there. And it wasn't until then that I realized why the tune he'd been playing sounded so familiar.

It was the guitar version of "Für Elise."

CHAPTER
Seven

HOW LONG DOES IT TAKE FOR SOMEONE TO stop grieving over a death anyway? One year? Two? Three? An entire life? Would the pain ever fade or would it always be there, a constant weight on my shoulders?

Unable to sleep, I watched as the moon sunk below the horizon and the sun rose. I got up early, unable to stand the stillness, the nothingness.

I waited until a half hour before school started and bought roses from the flower store that had just opened for the day. Proper flowers too. You know, the kind you get from those fancy stores where they wrap cellophane around the stems. They were a deep, passionate red—their color was stark against the white gravestone, so bright they were almost painful to look at. Many of the other graves were bare, their stones chipped, their facades peeling away to reveal a sadder, forgotten grave.

I couldn't bear that happening here.

I lingered near the graves until sunlight broke over the tops of the trees, and I knew it was time to head to school. The cemetery's wrought iron gates appeared in the mist before me just as a figure stepped out of the shadows to block my path. It was impossible not to recognize the golden-brown curls that framed a gaunt, arrogant face. I staggered back a few paces. My stomach twisted.

"Thought I'd find you here," Amanda said coldly. Two more figures stepped out from trees that lined the cemetery and stood beside her.

"I see you've brought your entourage," I muttered, acting braver than I felt. Riley's cropped red hair gleamed in the silvery light of the sun, and she was looking at me as someone might look at a slug. I was pretty sure the other girl's name was Abbey. Her skin was a deep, flawless brown, and the golden earrings and studs in her ears stood out against the darkness of her skin. Black curls spilled over her shoulders. She was sizing me up, watching me with her sharp, beady eyes. May was nowhere to be seen.

No one spoke.

I stared at my feet, unwilling to make eye contact with any of them, like the coward I am. "I'm sorry, Amanda, about before. I really don't know what got into me." I touched my hair, making sure it was covering my face.

"I don't want your apologies," she said.

I looked up at her. The angle of the sun cast a deep shadow across her face, but I could still make out the purplish bruise that swelled across her cheekbone and the stitched-up cut from the shattered glass that ran down her other cheek. Again, guilt stabbed at me. *Why* had I acted like that?

"Then go ahead, Amanda," I said. "Punch me. Knock me out. Whatever it is you want. Just get it over with."

"Maybe we don't want that either," drawled Riley.

"Then what *do* you want?"

A smile eased across Amanda's face. It stretched her gaunt, pale skin, making her look skeletal. She said, "We want to talk to you about Kesley."

Kesley? My mind blanked. Whatever I had been

expecting from them, this was *not* it. My stomach twisted into knots.

"I'm going to be late for school," I said flatly, turning to leave.

I should've known better than to turn my back on Amanda. "Who said you have a choice?" I heard her ask. There was a brief moment of silence when I halted, unsure, before the sound of something swished through the air before connecting with the back of my head. Pain lanced through my skull, hot and sharp, before my vision bled into darkness.

The rumble of an engine woke me.

It growled on and on, shuddering and spluttering as it was pushed to its limits. I tried to breathe, but something constricted my mouth. A gag, I realized. I shifted in my seat, but when I moved my hands and feet, a coarse, rough material chafed against my skin. Rope? A thick, black cloth covered my eyes, obscuring everything but a few flashes of color. *Green, brown, gold. Trees?* Panic engulfed me, the icy sort of fear that tightened my chest, shrouding all reasonable thought.

A throbbing pain centered at the back of my head.

My memories were a little confused, muddled. The last thing I remembered was encountering Amanda and her crew in the graveyard, then pain. How long had I been out? And where were they taking me?

Tears sprung into my eyes as I tried to suppress the panic.

"We're here," said a familiar voice. The car—or truck as it sounded—began to slow, groaning to an abrupt halt. "She's awake. Sweet Jesus, Jackson is going to kill me when he finds out."

"May, he's not going to find out," Amanda said from close by. I'd be a fool if I didn't hear the threat in her voice. "I'll make sure of that."

I struggled against my bonds to no avail. The sound of a truck door echoed, and then, much closer at hand, one opened. Fingers scrabbled at my hands and feet until the bonds loosened. The gag was pulled roughly from my mouth, and as I breathed in grate-fully, my nose was filled with the scent of pine needles and sweet, rotting leaves.

I jerked the black cloth from my eyes, the sudden bright light almost painful.

Scrambling out of the truck, I lurched forward, stumbling and crashing down. The reality of the situa-tion took a few seconds of frantic breathing to really sink in. I heard someone snicker, and a hand reached to grab me from the ground. "Let go!" I yelled, and my voice echoed around the clearing.

"No," snarled Amanda. "We're not—"

"You're hurting me. Let go—"

"Amanda," cut in a new voice. May. "Just leave her alone for a moment, okay? She can't go anywhere from here. We're two hours from Circling Pines. She can run, but it's not like she'd get far."

Amanda's grip loosened. I pulled myself away from her, pressing my back to the car in an attempt to get as far away from her as possible. But like May had said, where would I go? I barely registered my shaking hands, the beating of my heart. I forced in a deep breath and looked around me.

Golden trees stood proudly, leaves fluttering to the ground. And right there, nestled deep in the trees, was a wooden cabin with a thatched roof. Under any other circumstance, it would have looked cute. "Welcome to our humble abode," Amanda said dryly.

This was where they hung out? I looked at the four girls.

Amanda regarded me coolly, the barest hint of amusement glittering in her eyes. May stood more toward the truck, looking at me warily. Abbey and

Riley stood beside each other, gazes fixed on me as though they were daring me to run.

My hand flexed into a fist, nails biting into my palm.

I spoke, my voice scratchy with fear. "You told me you wanted to talk. So talk."

Amanda offered a smile that didn't touch her eyes. They remained as hard as the stones that littered the ground beneath her feet.

"Looks like you were right, May. She's not gonna run." She jerked her head to the cabin resting between the trees. "We'll talk in there, all right?"

I nodded, reluctantly following her through the trees. A minute later, Amanda had locked all five of us in the cabin. I didn't like this. Not one bit. I felt too trapped, suffocated.

The cabin looked no larger from the inside. It was empty except for a desk pushed up against the wall, one chair, and a wastebasket in the corner filled with candy wrappers and cigarette packs. As if on cue, Abbey pulled something from her pocket and a hissing sound rent the air as she lit her cigarette and took a drag.

May wrinkled her nose. She looked pointedly at Abbey. "In here? Gross."

She moved to one of the windows and yanked it

open. A rush of cool air swept in, but the sharp, stale scent of smoke lingered. My stomach clenched.

Riley snatched the cigarettes from Abbey's grip and lit one herself, her amber eyes and cropped hair gleaming in the sudden flare of the lighter. She saw me looking and said, "Want one?"

I shook my head.

Amanda yanked the pack from Riley, rolling her eyes and taking out a cigarette. "We are *so* not wasting these on her," she said as though I wasn't standing beside her. "They were such a bitch to get this time around."

Amanda puffed a cloud of smoke into my face, and I recoiled.

"That'll kill you one day, you know," I told her daringly.

She just laughed. "Yeah, I know that, genius. But you never know. I could be dead tomorrow morning anyway. Could be choked to death and thrown into a lake in the middle of fucking nowhere. I'm not worried about this."

"That's not funny," I hissed, anger licking at my insides, hot and ready to spill over. Amanda just shrugged. She flicked ash from the cigarette into the air, a trail of coiling smoke drifting through the cabin. She arched a brow at me as if she couldn't understand

why I was getting so worked up. She turned to Riley
and said, "Go on then. Tell her."

"Amanda, I'm not so sure this is a good idea…"
It was May who'd spoken. I'd almost forgotten she
was here. She'd just melted into the shadows, letting
the others take over. Vulnerability and uncertainty
pinched her features.

Amanda rounded on her, eyes glinting. "You got a
better one?"

I flinched at the harshness of her voice. I expected
May to recoil like I would have, but instead, she held
her ground. She was tougher than me. Her forest-
green eyes sharpened as she stared Amanda down.
Jackson and May both had the same determination, I
thought as I watched the two girls, and I almost felt a
smile curve at my lips.

Almost.

But then I remembered I was supposed to be at
school right now. And what was everyone going to
think when they found me missing? It wasn't like me
to cut school or do anything outside the rules. At least,
up until last week.

Finally, May relented. She graced Amanda with a
tight nod—a sign of begrudging acceptance—before
turning her back to the others in rebellion.

Amanda turned to Riley, who was now appraising me with an expression that told me she wasn't sure how I was going to react. Confusion knotted in my stomach, and I swallowed. What did they want to tell me?

Riley took another drag from her cigarette. "We want to figure out who killed Kesley," she said simply. I stared at her a few moments, taken aback.

"Why would you care?" I said. "She was my sister, not yours."

Abbey spoke up from the shadows. It was the first time she'd spoken since entering the cabin. "She was as much our sister as yours," she said softly, and the sincerity, the honesty in her voice frightened me.

"No," I said, now panicked, "she wasn't."

Riley's mouth curled into a scowl. "We're willing to help you, Ava, and you're going to turn down that opportunity? Amanda was right. You're stupider than you look." I shot Amanda a vicious look full of daggers.

She just shrugged.

I said, "Give me *one* good reason why you'd want to help me. You're nothing but trouble. Kesley would never have wasted her time with you."

From the shadows, Abbey laughed, a cigarette still

dangling from her lips. Her eyes had a wicked edge to them.

"Honey," said Amanda from beside me, "your sister was nothing *but* trouble. We had more in common than you probably think."

She's lying. That's what she does, said a small part of my mind.

The other part wasn't so sure.

"What do you mean?" I said. "She wasn't... She never would have—"

"Haven't you worked it out yet?" Amanda said, her voice harsh. When I just shook my head, she continued. "Kesley, K. Me, Amanda, A. Riley, R. May, M, and Abbey, A."

A terrible silence filled the cabin.

What she was telling me took a long time to reach my brain. At first, I thought I'd misheard her. Because I had to have, right? Everything I'd known—or *thought* I'd known—was turned on its head.

Each letter spelled out a member of their group.

K for Kesley.

Kesley.

She was part of their group.

She'd lied to me. Lied, lied, lied, lied. And her lies were beginning to stack up with each passing day.

Wasn't it ironic that the people standing in front of me right now were more honest than she'd ever been? I felt cheated, betrayed by her decision to confide in *them* but not me.

Liar, liar, blond hair on fire.

Dimly, I was aware of everyone staring at me, but I was too far away, locked in my own mind, to pay them much heed.

"Do you think she's going to pass out?" a voice whispered. May?

With a ragged, harsh breath, I drew myself back to the present and forced myself to act, to be strong. "Tell me everything," I said, surprising myself at how steady my voice had become with the pain still raging inside me.

Surprisingly, it was May who answered my demand.

"She started the group in our second year of high school, I think. She found us one by one, looking for people…like her, I guess."

"Like *her*?" I said, incredulous. "What's that supposed to mean?"

May just shrugged, saying, "Rebels. People who don't care whether they break the rules. People who needed to let loose."

"She found me first," Amanda butted in. She

tossed her hair over her shoulder, seemingly proud of this fact.

I narrowed my eyes. "She *found you*?"

"I had problems *way* before Kesley came along, sweetie. She just…heightened them. She wanted to form a group of people who were…"

"Troublemakers," I said through gritted teeth.

The ghost of a smile flickered across Amanda's face. "Call us what you will, hon. But compared to Kesley, we're nothing."

Another blow. I forced myself to say, "She was nothing like you."

"No," said Amanda softly, "you're right. She was worse. Way worse. You don't get it, do you? Everything we did, *she did*—we took the blame for it." She took a step forward, and it felt menacing. "And you wanna know why? Because *she* didn't want her perfect, golden reputation tarnished."

"No, she didn't. You're lying. You have to be."

Amanda's heated gaze flared with sudden hate. "God, Ava, don't be so *blind*! Your sister was a stinking, cowardly, pathetic excuse for a human being! She didn't *care* about any of us. She used us as a distraction, nothing more."

But a distraction from what?

"She wouldn't do that to you," I said, shaking my head. Then added, more to convince myself than the others, "*She wouldn't*. That's not the Kesley I know."

"Maybe that's not the Kesley you knew," May said quietly, "but that's the Kesley she *was*."

"*Shut up!*" As soon as the words left my mouth, I got my wish. A tightly coiled silence filled the room, squeezing the breath from my lungs and tightening the tension in the cabin that was already stretched to the breaking point. It took a few moments for the inferno of rage inside me to dull down to a blaze. When I spoke again, every word shook. I didn't even care. "If my sister was such a bitch to you all, then why do you want to help me?"

"Because she's dead," snapped Amanda.

The bluntness of her words cut through me. Ever since Kesley's funeral, people had been dancing around those words as if they feared my reaction. Oddly, Amanda's words seemed to ground me, and something slotted into place in my mind.

"You think Kesley was killed because she created KARMA, and you think one of you might be next."

It wasn't a question, but May responded anyway. "Yes."

"Can you blame whoever killed her?" I asked,

feeling a stab of vindictive pleasure at the hurt that
flashed across May's face. She shrank back into the
shadows once more, invisible. She looked frail,
diminished, and for the first time, I noticed the
circles under her eyes. As if she hadn't been sleeping much.

Well, I thought, *that makes two of us.*

And I still didn't feel the need to apologize to her.

Amanda took over the reins. She seemed unaffected
by what I'd just said, not that I was surprised. "That's
not the point, okay? We want to know who did this to
Kesley so it won't happen again."

"But who else knew?" I asked. "*I* didn't, and
neither does the rest of Circling Pines. She was never
questioned by the police, never sent to juvie."

"If we knew," said Amanda, looking at me as if I
were an idiot, "we wouldn't be talking to you right
now, would we?"

I met her gaze unflinchingly. "I'm not saying I
believe you," I said. "But if you hated the way my
sister treated you, then why didn't you just stop?"

Abbey laughed from the shadows, and it was a cold,
black sound. She said, "We tried. A couple times. But
Kesley had a way of making you see things her way.
And what was the point anyway? She made us feel...

together. Like we had a place. Like we were actually worth something."

Amanda said softly, "And besides, Ava, who would've believed us? Say we *did* tell someone about Kesley and what she'd done. It's a criminal's word against hers. Who would *you* believe?" My silence gave Amanda all the answer she needed. "Kesley was twisted but smart. She knew that either way, we had no choice but to go along with what she wanted."

That didn't sound like Kesley, not at *all*. Not my Kesley. Not the protector, not the one I knew and loved with my entire heart.

My gaze searched the four girls. They were all watching me, as if waiting for something. I realized I was twisting my hands together, and they were slippery with sweat.

"Okay," I said a little breathlessly. "You want me to join you."

Abbey's eyebrows shot up, but beside me, Amanda looked satisfied. "Yeah," she said. "Something like that anyway. We want you to help us."

I bit my lip. "I don't know…"

"Look, honey," said Amanda. "You haven't got much of a choice here." She took another cigarette and motioned to Abbey, who passed the lighter to her grudgingly. One she'd lit up, Amanda took a long drag, and smoke billowed from her mouth.

"Give her a *choice*," May said. "She deserves that at least."

Amanda cast her a flat look.

"Well, of course she doesn't *have* to do anything," Riley said in a low drawl. "But, Ava, she *was* your sister. You owe it to her to find her killer."

But for whose benefit? Mine or theirs? Her gaze was steady as she looked at me. "You know she'd have done the same for you."

Would she have?

The thought passed through my mind unbidden. Surely, Kesley, my sister, my protector, would have done what I was doing for her? But this, *this*, opened up a whole new alley of questions—ones that made me question her. How could I honestly say she would still protect me after the things I'd just learned?

"I have eyes, Ava," May whispered, her voice low and urgent. "I see the looks people give us. Give *me*. What if someone discovered Kesley's involvement in what we were doing? What do you think would have happened to her?"

I dropped my gaze, staring at the floor. What she said *made sense*, even though part of me—a *large* part of me—didn't want to believe it. And that wasn't even the worst part. None of them *cared*. None of them sought the closure I did. All Amanda, May, Riley, and Abbey wanted was to make sure *they* wouldn't be the next target.

So where did that leave me?

They were staring at me, waiting for an answer. I glanced around at them and realized I didn't really have an option. Amanda was right. If I didn't join, she was going to find some way to obliterate all happiness from my life, and May was staring at me with such an imploring expression that I spoke before I realized I'd made up my mind.

"Okay," I said. "What do you want me to do?"

—————

Apparently, I'd earned enough trust not to be blindfolded on the way back. Not that I could have said where their cabin was anyway. The highway pretty much looked the same the whole way to me. Trees and asphalt.

Circling Pines was quiet when we arrived. The leaves lay lifeless on the ground, a wind rattling though the trees and lifting my hair. The truck screeched away as soon as Amanda let me out of the vehicle. School was out and had probably been for some time. I made my way to campus anyway, knowing that if I didn't, my presence in detention was going to be missed.

I walked through the corridors in a daze.

I wanted nothing more than to lie in bed, staring at the sunlit-striped ceiling, and digest what I'd found out. A tiredness that hadn't been there this morning lingered inside me.

A teacher was already present when I pushed open the detention door.

She looked over her thick-rimmed glasses, glanced down at her list, and jerked her head to the array of waiting seats. At least half of them were filled with very bored-looking students, who were chewing gum or scratching profanities on desks. "Nice of you to join us, Miss Hale."

I said nothing.

A few students raised their heads, but I managed to get to the other side of the classroom without too much unwanted scrutiny. A dark-haired figure caught my attention, sitting just outside the teacher's view at the far side of the room. When the teacher stood up to shut the door as noisy students passed, I took that as my opportunity to slide from my seat and join Rafe.

"What are you doing here?" I whispered.

"I could ask you the same thing," he said, his voice low.

"I have detention."

He arched an eyebrow at me. "Yeah, so do I. Apparently smoking on school grounds is against the rules. Did you know that?"

I didn't for a second believe he thought smoking on school grounds was allowed. "I thought you'd stopped that."

Rafe shot me a "get real" sort of look. He said, "So where have you been for the past day?"

"I don't know," I said, fumbling over my words. Why hadn't I figured out an adequate excuse by now? "Just places."

"Places? That's funny."

"What?" I snapped.

"None of KARMA was here today either."

I felt my cheeks fill with heat, but I kept my expression stoic. "So? They're not here most days," I said.

"But you are," he countered. "You're always here, no matter what."

"Look," I said patiently. "It really doesn't matter."

"Was this about Kesley?"

I just stared at him, silent. What should I tell him?

Was it possible that he already knew more than I did? But it was too late—my silence was enough of an answer for him.

I was saved from speaking when the teacher noticed our whispered conversation. "Is there a problem here?"

I didn't even look up and instead let Rafe answer for us.

"All good," he said. I could imagine the charming smile that he flashed at her, dazzling her into not reprimanding either of us further.

The moments trickled past so slowly that I had to wonder whether our teacher had disabled the classroom clock. I cast Rafe sidelong glances every few minutes, but he didn't seem interested in saying anything else. He drummed his fingers on the table and looked out the window.

I traced my eyes over the sharp line of his jaw. Was it wrong to want to run my fingers along his jawline when I had a boyfriend? I fiddled with my hair and looked away. Of course it was.

I told myself to focus on something else, something that *wasn't* Rafe, so I stared at the backs of the chairs instead, reading the words carved there. One in particular caught my eye. A love heart was drawn there with two names written inside: *Jackson and Kesley.*

After all I'd learned today, why was I even surprised?

I was out the door before I could think things through. I heard the teacher call after me in a loud, authoritative voice, but I paid no heed as I rushed through the corridors, my tears making it hard to see.

In the bathroom, I splashed water over my face.

The cold helped clear my mind. Maybe I was overreacting. Maybe someone had put the heart there as a joke. Maybe what I was thinking couldn't be true.

All I had to do was collect my thoughts and I'd go back there…right? But that was proving difficult as the reality of the situation sunk in.

I wiped a hand across my face, feeling the roughness of my scar, the wetness of my tears.

Kesley and Jackson.

I was sick of this. Sick of it. Everything I had ever thought about my sister was crashing down around me. How could I live with someone for sixteen years but feel like I didn't know her at all? Keeping secrets, I realized, was a bit of an art.

One wrong move, like choosing to sit near *that chair*, could unravel them all. And I couldn't help but wonder: what would I think of her when I'd unwound them all?

I only looked up when someone touched my shoulder.

It was a gentle touch, but it still made me flinch like I'd been shocked. "Sorry," Rafe said quietly. I wondered *what* in particular he was sorry about.

What had he seen?

The look on his face told me he'd seen enough. I meant to tell him to leave, but instead, all that came out was, "This is a girls' bathroom."

"Yeah, I can already feel my masculinity falling." A beat of silence. And then, "I'm sorry. I had no idea. Kesley never told me."

"I guess there were a lot of things about my sister I didn't know."

Rafe met my gaze in the mirror, his eyes blue and warm. "Everyone has secrets," he said. "Some are just…bigger than others, I guess."

I raised an eyebrow. "And what are yours?"

"You still believe I harmed your sister?"

"I just found out Kesley may have had an affair with my boyfriend. I don't know what to believe anymore."

He shrugged. "Fair enough. Trust is complicated. I get that."

"Tell me then," I said softly.

"Tell you what?"

"Your secrets."

"Oh well."

He folded his arms across his chest. "Promise not to laugh?"

I was intrigued now. "Yeah, sure."

"You remember first grade, Valentine's Day?"

I scrunched up my face, trying to remember. "Not really."

Rafe shoved his hands deep into his pockets. "Mrs. Steep made us send a valentine to one person in the class."

"Yeah, and…?"

"I was way too chicken to sign it with my name."

My brow furrowed. "So…that's it? That's your big secret?"

He laughed, and the sound echoed off the bathroom walls. "No, not entirely. I've never told *anyone* who I sent it to."

"Who? Oh, Kesley?" How was this supposed to make me feel better?

A smile twitched on Rafe's face. "No, Ava, I didn't. Am I going to have to spell it out? I sent it to *you*."

I didn't need to be staring at the mirror to know my cheeks were flushed with embarrassment. "*Oh*. Oh. Me? You sent your first-grade Valentine to me? Why me out of everyone there?"

Rafe tilted his head to the side as if he were thinking,

eyes twinkling. "I thought you were pretty. Long blond hair and all," he said.

That stung. "Were? As in I'm not anymore?"

I thought it was strange he would say something like that. That was the year everything started. My parents dying, being brought up in foster care, and... well, that was the year of the accident too.

You tended to stand out when you were the only kid with half her face burned off. The scars had been red and angry back then, instead of dulled like now. No one had said it, but I knew what they'd been thinking.

What happened to your face?

Rafe's smile turned into a grin. "No, that's not what I was saying at all. I just didn't think it prudent to say so while you still have a boyfriend."

The mention of Jackson made my stomach curl in. "Well," I murmured, walking to the door, "by the end of the day, I'm not sure I will anymore."

———

The moment I was released from detention, I texted Jackson.

He replied instantly, asking if I wanted a ride home, and I stood there, just outside the school gates, staring at the message. Did I? I needed to talk to him about what happened, but a part of me—the weak, cowardly part—still wanted to forget everything I'd seen.

But I couldn't do that.

I needed to know the truth, however bitter and horrible it was. Besides, who said there *wasn't* a logical, non-cheating answer to all this?

But even *I* couldn't fool myself into believing that.

I answered, asking him to meet me at the local park and saying that we needed to talk. Then I switched off my phone without waiting for his response.

The park was empty. Completely, utterly empty. Not even any children were there. The sun was hidden by the surrounding trees, casting most of the park in deep shadows. It was nearing late afternoon, and no parent would want their child out in a park just before nightfall. Not with a killer on the loose.

The park screamed of neglect. Weeds fought through the cracks in the pavement, rust lingered stubbornly on the play equipment, and the scent of loneliness seemed to cling to the air. A lamp flickered on almost above me, casting a golden sheen of light across the springy grass. A few wooden benches were scattered around the park, but I was too anxious to sit down. Nerves hummed through me, mixed with dread and the slightest bit of hope—which I squashed down instantly.

A shadow stepped into the light. "Jackson," I whispered.

He reached forward and pressed a kiss to my right cheek, not giving me time to pull away. "Hey, babe—"

"Were you...*with* my sister?" The words came out quick and sharp, a tumble of unidentified emotions. I was glad I hadn't stalled. If this were heading where I thought it was, I wanted it done quickly, like ripping off a Band-Aid. Silence followed, broken only by birds that chirped in the nearby trees.

"Ava," Jackson said slowly.

"Just answer the question."

Most of his face was in the shadow cast by the lengthening night, so it was hard to read his face properly. "It was a long time ago," he said.

"So it's true? It's true you and Kesley were—"

"A long time ago—"

"—together behind my back..." I let my voice trail off into nothing, let it drift onto the wind as another breeze encircled the park. "Oh."

My mind felt frozen, confused, unable to digest what he had just told me. I'd expected him to deny it. To laugh it off and tell me that it wasn't true, that he loved me. But no, he'd told me the truth. And that truth hurt like hell. What was that expression? Ignorance was indeed bliss.

I did the only rational thing my mind could conjure up.

I burst into tears.

Jackson didn't come any closer or wrap his arms around me. He didn't tell me everything was going to be okay. In fact, when I had cried as much as I could, I looked up. He was nowhere to be seen.

I wasn't sure which scared me most: finding out that Kesley was part of Circling Pines's most infamous gang, my mother yelling at me when she discovered I'd cut school for the day, or unraveling the secret of Kesley's and my boyfriend's relationship. Right now, halfway through my mother's furious lecture, all three choices were running pretty close.

"You had me worried *sick*," Diana was saying, slamming down the chopping board on the counter. "I was literally minutes away from calling the police!"

"Sorry," I whispered. How many times did someone have to apologize before their meaning became true?

I fell into a chair and stared at the marble countertop. Half a minute of painful silence followed.

"Are you okay, dear?" I glanced up to see her looking at me as if she'd just noticed my red and puffy eyes. When I didn't say anything, she sighed. "I'm sorry if I made you upset, but—"

"It wasn't you," I said, wiping my face. That proved pointless because the tears had already dried, leaving nothing but a stinging residue behind.

"Oh, sweetheart, what's wrong?" Her hostile tone melted as concern overrode it. She edged around the countertop and sat down next to me, pushing away some of the strands of hair to see me better.

"Is this about Kesley again?" she asked softly.

I just nodded, letting the hair fall over my face to create a comfortable curtain between us. "I think you should talk to someone," she suggested.

"It's not because she's dead," I whispered. "It's because of what she *did*."

There was a beat of silence. "What did she do?"

"She—" I coughed, clearing my throat, and started again. "She was in a relationship with Jackson."

"While he was with you?"

I nodded, sniffing.

My mother wrapped her arms around me. "She

made a mistake. Everyone makes mistakes. You know that. But she's gone now, Ava, and...I'm sure some part of her regretted what she'd done."

"She never told me," I said, tears leaking out the corner of my eyes.

"She was probably afraid," my mother said gently. "She knew telling you would have hurt you more." A pause. And then, "Does Jackson know you know?"

"Yeah," I said.

"Do you think you could forgive him? Do you think you *should* forgive him?"

"I hope so." I did, didn't I?

She drew back to look at me, her fingers lingering on my roughened, scarred cheek. "I'm not going to tell you what you should do. That's entirely up to you. But if he can't see how truly amazing you are, then he's not worth your time." Typical mother line, but all the same, it did make me feel better.

My mother looked at me, eyes gleaming. Was she crying?

"We'll get through this, Ava," she said. "One day at a time."

Part of me wished I could have told her something more, something about the things I had learned today and the turmoil lashing against my insides. I didn't though. Despite the fact I loved Diana, she was not my mother. There had always been a chasm that couldn't be bridged. She tried, she really did, but the hours she spent at work had taken their toll, long before she realized it was happening.

So did that make it my fault too?

I hadn't really known my birth mother. But that had never stopped me from clinging to her memory.

I closed my eyes briefly, breathing out a slow sigh and pulling myself together enough to help with dinner, pretending, pretending, pretending everything was okay when it was not.

I don't think Diana noticed.

So I excused myself after barely touching my dinner and shut myself in my room. Sleep sounded like a brilliant idea, confirmed by the aching in my temples, but too many thoughts were rattling around in my head. It felt like a tornado of emotions tangled together so tightly that it was difficult to tell them apart. Anger. Frustration. Guilt. Sadness.

Anger at the lies I'd been fed. Lies I knew I'd believed.

Frustration at not seeing Kesley for who she was.

Guilt at the ever-growing distance between Diana and me.

And sadness for all the things I had thought were true.

I stared at the ceiling. Glow-in-the-dark stars shone there, casting a wan light over the room and making my skin look pallid. I curled my hands into fists, my breathing becoming tighter and tighter. Hot tears strained to be released behind my eyes. "I *hate* you, Kesley," I whispered.

And then I cried myself to sleep.

Not only have you tarnished so many beautiful recollections I had of you, but the choices you made twisted them, turning them into something ugly.

Each memory I had of you was gilded with gold, something I've learned was only a guise. And peeling that facade away, strip by aching strip, revealed a new, more accurate image. Gone was the sister I had looked up to so adoringly. And in her place stood a crueler, heartless sister. One who hadn't been afraid to hurt, steal, and lay blame on others. Were there any signs that should have warned me about the colder girl lying just beneath your skin? Because sometimes, it was just easier to believe the beautiful lie rather than the truth.

So, congratulations, Kesley, you had me fooled from the beginning. But you know what the worst part was?

I didn't hate you. Couldn't.

Not even after I found out about KARMA. Not even after I found out about Jackson.

And even now as I'm writing this, after everything that has happened, I can't hate you. I can't. You're not supposed to think ill of the dead, because how are they supposed to defend themselves? But what if they'd done something so

bad, so awful that you had to think ill of them?
That you needed to.

What if...

Eight

IT WAS IMPOSSIBLE TO ESCAPE MY thoughts, no matter how hard I tried. As soon as I reached school the next day and saw Rafe standing at the gates, I walked right up to him. "Jackson told me the truth," I said by way of greeting.

Rafe turned, his eyes widening in surprise. Whether from seeing me there or Jackson telling the truth, I didn't know. "Which was what?" he asked, running a hand through his hair and rumpling it.

"I was right," I said softly. This time, admitting the truth didn't make me feel like crying.

Rafe held my gaze. "I'm sorry," he said.

Don't be, I wanted to tell him. *It's not your fault.* But then whose fault was it? Mine? Jackson's? Maybe we were all to blame.

Perhaps something of my thoughts showed on my face, because Rafe asked, "Are you going to talk to him?"

"Who? Jackson?" I considered it for a moment.

"Well, yes." His eyes glinted. "There's always more than one side to a story, you know."

I don't know if he was talking about more than Jackson or if I was imagining that. Maybe I was just connecting everything I heard to Kesley.

But maybe Rafe was right. Maybe I *should* talk to Jackson. After all, I hadn't given him much of a chance to talk. I nodded, scarcely paying attention.

I'd be lying if I said there wasn't the vaguest bit of hope in Rafe's expression.

And I had no idea what that was supposed to mean.

———

I found Jackson not ten minutes later.

He was waiting for me under the ancient maple tree, its roots cracking the concrete as they rose from the ground. Jackson was pacing—back and forth, back and forth—his brows narrowed, his lips pinched in an expression of deep thought. As I watched, a leaf fluttered to the ground.

He looked genuinely upset, but what did that mean? Was he sorry for what he had done or just sorry because I'd caught him?

"Hey," I called.

Jackson turned, the agitation that had sharpened his features melting into a smile. But his smile faded when I didn't return it.

"Hey, Ava." Jackson chose to go with the nonchalant approach. You know, hands in his pockets, blank expression. Not that it mattered; I'd gotten a glimpse of what he really felt a moment before. "Let me explain," he said, his voice uncharacteristically quiet.

"Go on," I said harshly. "Explain."

"I would've last night," he started, "but you wouldn't have listened."

"So, what? You just left me there instead?"

"You didn't look to be in a forgiving mood," he tried, his voice almost pleading.

"I'm not now either."

He grimaced and ran his hands through his hair, which was gleaming gold in the early morning sunlight. Then he took my hand without asking and tugged me deeper into the shade of the trees, the darkness making it harder to see his face. I couldn't help wondering if he'd done that on purpose. But people were hovering around the tree, so maybe he just wanted privacy.

I pulled my hand away from his grip.

"Fine," I said. "I'm listening."

"I was with Kesley when you and I started dating," he said flatly. No emotion, no feeling—just stating the facts.

"Oh, why didn't you say so?" I said. "I guess that makes it all right then."

"No, babe," he said, reaching for my hands again but halting when I flinched, "that's not what I'm saying at all."

"Then what *are* you saying, Jackson? Because I don't understand."

This time, when he leaned forward to take my hand, I let him, feeling the warmth of his skin sink into mine. "Look, like I said, you and I had just gotten together. And it was just that you weren't there one afternoon, and she was. It was one time, and—"

I flinched. I did *not* need to hear that. I fought the childish desire to cover my ears. "Stop," I said. "Just stop right there. You carved your names into a freaking chair! What was I supposed to think?"

"What do you mean?"

"I found a chair in the detention room," I said. "It had… It had Kesley's and your names carved into its back. That's how I found out."

Jackson's hands tightened a little around mine. "I didn't do that," he promised. "Kesley must have…" He let his voice trail off.

Of course. Why would I have thought it was Jackson? It didn't seem like him to flaunt a relationship in front of me.

"But I didn't love her, Ava," Jackson said after a silence. "I promise. It was always you. *Always.* If I could take it all back, I would. It was a mistake."

"Okay," I said mechanically.

"Okay?" Jackson echoed. "Does that mean we can…you know, start over?" He sounded hopeful. I didn't have the heart to burst his bubble.

Truth be told, I didn't know what I felt. Every emotion inside me had been stretched to its limit last night, pulling my chest so tightly that I could barely breathe. Yet I felt lighter now than when I'd walked through the school gates this morning. Happier somehow.

Did that mean I'd forgiven him?

Jackson was looking at me, and I could almost imagine his pale-green eyes wide and pleading, much like his sister's. For a moment, I was brought back to the cabin and the deal I'd struck with *them*. Looking at May then, you wouldn't have thought she'd hurt a fly, but she'd done just as many awful things as Amanda had. So where did that leave Jackson? Was he as innocent as he looked and sounded?

He had said it was a *mistake*. Fine. But I wouldn't forget this, because every new piece of information I was uncovering about Kesley drew me closer to understanding why she was killed.

Maybe, just maybe, the killer had had enough of her behavior too.

———

After detention, I met Lia for coffee.

She eyed me over the rim of her coffee cup. "You're insane, Ava. You know that, right? He, like, *cheated* on you, and you're just taking him back? Just like that?" Lia snapped her fingers together for emphasis. She flipped her black, shiny hair, eyes narrowing.

Okay, so maybe my best friend had a valid point,

but I hadn't forgiven Jackson completely. Our relationship still felt cracked, as if any small impact would shatter it entirely. But I wasn't going to tell Lia that though.

She raised a neatly sculpted eyebrow, waiting for a reply.

"I don't know," I said. "I guess I love him."

We'd been together for so long that it was hard to imagine *not* loving Jackson. He was the comfortable choice. The one I would go back to, again and again. But was that sort of love worth staying for?

Lia stared fixedly at me for a few more moments, and I felt my cheeks warm under her scrutiny. Was she trying to see if I was being honest with her? Suddenly, I wasn't sure I wanted to know what she saw in my expression. Truth? Lies? Finally, she changed the subject, prattling on about something I was only half listening to. I was too distracted; Jackson still crowded my thoughts.

A flurry of activity in the doorway made me straighten as a gentle chime rang through the coffee shop. Two familiar figures had stepped into the shop: Amanda, with her wild, golden curls, and May, who kept her head low and a hood pulled over her face. They turned to our table.

Oh boy.

Lia had realized my attention was focused somewhere else. She'd cut off midsentence and glanced over her shoulder. Her hand instinctively clenched into a fist. "What are they *doing*?" she hissed. "And why are they coming *here*?"

My heart pounded. I looked into the depths of my coffee cup, wishing I could drown in it. Why couldn't they just leave me alone?

"You can't sit here," Lia said boldly as they neared our table.

Amanda ignored her entirely and slipped into the leather seat beside me. May sat opposite, blocking the street view.

"We need to talk," Amanda said.

Lia was silent. She was just staring at Amanda and May with a slightly open mouth. My best friend could be outspoken sometimes, but she wasn't stupid.

"Later," I said coldly. *Not in front of Lia*, was what I didn't add.

"No, *now*," said Amanda. "You told us you'd help, so we expect you to follow through."

I closed my eyes but not before I saw confusion knot Lia's forehead.

Glee flickered across Amanda's face before she said,

voice drawling, "*Oh*. You haven't told Lia, have you? Keeping her in the dark, are we?"

I'd promised to help them, but oh no, that wasn't enough for Amanda. She had to humiliate me in front of my best friend too.

I stared at my cup again and said nothing.

"Ava," Lia said, "what are they talking about?"

"Nothing," I whispered, but it sounded false even to my ears.

"*Ava*," Amanda mimicked in a cruel imitation of Lia's slightly whiny tone, "*what are they talking about?*" Her lip curled, and she focused her attention on me.

If I involved Lia in Kesley's twisted tale, there was no telling how much she would get hurt. I cared for her, and what if this thing with Kesley became too dangerous?

I took a deep breath and turned to Lia. This was not going to be pleasant. "We'll talk later, all right?"

Lia's face turned cold. Blank. Emotionless. Her flawless skin and wide eyes made her look like a porcelain doll—flat and lifeless. She grabbed her bag from the seat and stood up. "Don't bother," she said, then left.

I closed my eyes, only opening them when I was sure Lia had gone.

"You didn't have to be so cruel, Amanda," said May.

Amanda just lifted a shoulder as if to say, *So what?* To me, she said, "We're sorry about you and Jackson."

"We haven't broken up."

"Yeah, but it must've been *hard*. I mean," Amanda continued, "what do you think would have happened if Kesley were still alive?"

What would have happened? Jackson and I had been together for almost two years. I knew him…or at least I thought I did. I knew his favorite color was deep blue. I knew he hated the cold and devoured the warmth. But how had I not known something so integral to our relationship as that he'd been involved with my sister? For all I knew, Jackson's feelings for Kesley *had* developed over time. For all I knew, he'd thought of her when we kissed or touched. Amanda's implication that he would have fallen for Kesley again stung—and not because it was unlikely.

I felt a stab of self-pity. It was terrible to envy a dead girl, but I couldn't help it.

"Spit it out, Amanda," I said. "What are you getting at?"

"I'll tell you, but you won't like it," she said.

What a shocker. I'd learned so many heartbreaking

things in the past twenty-four hours that I wasn't sure it was possible to be surprised anymore.

I gave Amanda a hard look. "Go on, tell me."

"We know who might have killed her," May said, her voice soft.

"You know who killed her?" I asked, breathless. I felt as if my lungs were shrinking, and no matter how many breaths I took, they would never be enough.

Amanda raised an eyebrow at me scathingly. "If I knew who killed her, I wouldn't be in a coffee shop. I'd been in the police station, idiot."

She had a point. "So then, who do you think killed her?"

"None of us knew about Kesley and Jackson."

"So?" I said. "Neither did I. Or anyone else for that matter."

Amanda ground her teeth. "You don't get it, do you? She told us everything. *Everything*. Why would she want to hide that from us?"

I couldn't help my bitter laugh. "Funny, isn't it? She knew everything about you, but you knew *nothing* about her." There was a long, stretched silence in which I realized I'd said the wrong thing. Amanda's eyes gleamed dangerously, and even May went white. "Sorry," I said, my voice quiet and small.

May was the first to recover. She shook her head. "Forget it. Anyway," she continued, "Amanda and I…we had an idea. About Kesley and Jackson."

I eyed her curiously. "Yeah?"

May took a deep breath, then said, "Every murder needs a motive, right? What if… What if it was Jackson, Ava? I mean, there must have been a reason she didn't tell us about their relationship. What if Kesley *did* want to tell someone, but Jackson killed her before she could?"

Horror churned in my stomach. "May, he's your *brother*."

May recoiled.

"It checks out," said Amanda, and as usual, her voice was emotionless. "What better way to silence someone than kill them?"

"Because Jackson wouldn't do something like that," I whispered. "I know him. It's not… He wouldn't…"

Amanda's lips twisted into a smile. She said, "Funny, isn't it? You think you know someone, but then something happens, something small—or big, it doesn't matter—and you're forced to reconsider everything you've ever known about them."

I knew her words were in retaliation for my earlier comment, but they still burned because she had a point.

"It's just a hunch," May said quickly, as if sensing the growing tension.

"No," Amanda snapped, "it isn't just a *hunch*. It makes sense. Perfect sense. Kesley felt guilty about their relationship. She wanted to tell you, but Jackson wouldn't like that, would he? So he strangled her to shut her up."

The connection there was not lost on me.

Her words brought a flurry of unpleasant images into my head: a rope, a lake, a body. A tingle of doubt was growing in the corner of my mind, but I pushed it back. *No.* There was no chance Jackson would've ever done something like that. Right? I looked at May, incredulous. She had slunk down in her seat, not looking at me. "I can't believe you're even considering this, May! You *know* Jackson would never do something like this. I know you do."

She frowned and met my gaze grudgingly. "No, Ava, I don't," she said. "A few days ago, I never would've thought he'd cheat on you. Ever. But now? I don't know what to think."

I blinked back tears. "Cheating is one thing, but murder...?"

"Most murders aren't planned," said Amanda. "Who's saying this wasn't a heat-of-the-moment thing?"

"This one wasn't," I insisted, grasping at wisps of information. "Whoever it was, Kesley must have trusted them if she was willing to go all the way to Lake O'Hara, right? If Jackson *had* killed her, why would he bother with all that? Why would he go to those lengths? Wouldn't he have killed her wherever?"

My own words sent a thrill of fear through me, because until that moment, I hadn't realized just how true they were. With what Rafe had told me and finding out about the self-defense lessons, it made sense. I didn't care what May or Amanda thought. I didn't. This had been careful, meticulous, no clues left behind. And that made the situation more sinister—because it would be so easy to stare into the eyes of a killer and not even know it.

May and Amanda were both eyeing me with pity, as if they thought I was clinging to some false hope. I couldn't sit there a moment longer.

I stood up, fists clenching. "You're wrong. Both of you. I don't care what you say, what you think, because Jackson had nothing to do with this. Nothing. And besides, *Jackson* ended it with *Kesley*. Not the other way around. So what motivation would he have to kill her?"

They were silent. That was answer enough for me, so I threw some change on the table as a tip and left.

I walked home, letting the crisp night air kiss my cheeks.

Like May, I would never have thought Jackson capable of cheating on me. But that had been flipped upside down in a day, so why couldn't he be capable of murder? *People are so strangely complex*, I thought.

Diana greeted me with a cup of hot chocolate when I got home.

I sank into a chair at the table. The walk home wasn't long, but it was nice to wrap my hands around something warm, letting it bleed into my skin. "Thanks, Diana," I murmured.

She clucked her tongue. "You know I hate it when you call me that."

I shrugged but didn't say anything. Sometimes, like today, it just felt *wrong* to call her my mother.

She cleared her throat. "So, you were at the coffee shop all evening?"

All evening? I frowned and glanced at the clock. It was almost six o'clock; I hadn't realized I'd been that long. I shrugged again and said, "I guess so."

"But you're certain you were there all evening? And with someone?"

I narrowed my eyes at her. Why was she being so obtrusive? I forced myself to answer in a calm, even tone. "*Yes*, I'm sure. I met up with Lia after school. We had coffee, and I came home." My mother breathed out a sigh, seemingly satisfied with my answer.

She reached over and touched my cheek, my unscarred cheek, gently. "I just worry about you, Ava. You've been through so much. Too much."

"I know," I said, feeling strangely emotionless. *Sometimes, I worry about me too*. But I didn't say this. It would worry her more. So I only smiled, took a sip of hot chocolate to warm my throat, and stared out into the dark.

I woke to frost. It braided across the bottom of my window in intricate patterns, reminiscent of a spider-web. A *plink, plink* on the window had pulled me from sleep. I wrapped as much blanket around myself as I could, walked to the window, and lifted the latch.

Cold air blasted in, and I shivered. Gray dawn light leaked through the clouds, and the sun hadn't woken yet.

"Rise and shine," said a sarcastic voice from below me.

I looked down. Rafe was standing there, looking as though he'd been awake for hours. A guitar was slung over his shoulder. I groaned and pressed my head to the windowpane. "Why are you even here? It's early."

Rafe shrugged with the ghost of a smile. "Not to someone who's had their coffee."

"You didn't answer my question," I said, shivering again.

"I wanted to talk about Kesley," he said, a guarded expression crossing his face.

"All right," I said. "Do you want to come in?"

He paused for a moment. "How about we go for a walk?"

I glanced at the gray rain clouds and hesitated, then nodded, telling him I'd be downstairs in a few minutes. I got dressed, put a beanie on my head, tied a scarf around my neck, and went to open the door.

"Ready?" Rafe asked. He shouldered the guitar more firmly. The strap was worn yet dusty, so the guitar seemed to be a favorite that had been neglected lately. Ten minutes later, we found ourselves at the park.

Frost clung to the grass and crunched underfoot as I followed Rafe up the twisty, windy path that led behind the park and deeper into the woods.

I wondered if I should be more afraid.

We trekked silently through the woods for several minutes. It was so early that even the birds had yet to rise and so cold that my breath misted with every exhale. Rafe stopped at a clearing where patches of silvery sunlight touched the ground.

"I came here with Kesley," said Rafe, breaking the silence.

"Oh. How romantic."

I sat on the grass, feeling its cold touch through my clothes. I didn't need to look at Rafe to know he was smiling.

"You know I never felt like that about her."

"I believe you now," I said. "And besides, she was probably too busy screwing my boyfriend." Even the words tasted bitter in my mouth.

Rafe plucked a few notes on his guitar. "Yet you're still with him."

I looked away, wanting to change the subject.

I nodded at the guitar and said, "Is that what you want to do after graduation? Be a musician?"

"No, I don't think so. I love it, but it's a hobby not a passion. Ideally, I want to work with people, to help them. Maybe I'll get a degree in psychology."

A psychology degree? A strange choice for Rafe.

"Why did you bring the guitar here anyway?"

He said, "It reminds me of Kesley. She played the piano like a pro, but she struggled with guitar. So I offered to teach her. After school mainly, we'd come down here for an hour or two." Rafe smirked. "She wanted to go somewhere people wouldn't hear how terrible she was at it."

I couldn't help but smile. But then I thought back to the music store and that phone call I'd made. I tilted my head in Rafe's direction. "Did you know she was talking about taking self-defense lessons?"

Rafe said, "She mentioned it."

I let out a small sound of disbelief, but why was I even surprised?

"And you didn't think you should *tell* me this?"

He turned to me, his eyes narrowed. "Let's say I did tell you. What would you have done about it? What would even the police do with something like that?"

I didn't answer him. The truth was, I didn't know. And this wasn't about the police doing something. It was about me feeling *worthy* to know Kesley's secrets. Was that a selfish thing to keep thinking? Everyone had their secrets, so why was it so important I know hers?

Rafe turned to me. "Ava," he said so gently that I allowed myself to look at him. "It wasn't about shutting you out, I promise. It never was. Remember what I said—that she thought someone was after her?" I nodded. "She loved you more than anything else in this world…and I think—I think she just wanted to keep you from all that." I felt my jaw automatically clench. And here it was again: that feeling that he was dancing around something.

Only this time, I thought I was closer to the truth than before.

"Didn't work very well, did it?" I said with a sad, ironic smile. I lay back on the grass, ignoring the cold and focusing instead on the patches of brightening sky visible through the trees. "It doesn't matter anymore what she was trying to do, Rafe. I'm—*we're*—in this, no matter how much she tried to keep it from me, and I'm determined to see this to its end." I turned my head slightly to look at him. "And I *need* you to be honest with me."

An unreadable expression glinted in his eyes. "That goes both ways."

I felt a brief flicker of frustration at his words. Hadn't I been anything *but* honest with him? He was the one keeping secrets from *me*.

Not the other way round.

I sat up. "Fine," I said. "So tell me what you know."

"Most of it you already know," Rafe said, shrugging.

"But not all of it," I insisted, heart racing. Was I finally going to get some answers? Nerves twisted in my stomach.

"No, not all of it," he said, his gaze impassive. "For example, I never told you what Kesley did in her downtime."

A moment passed, and then I said, "KARMA."

He knew about that? Of *course* he knew about that.

"When did they tell you?" I asked him.

"Soon after I got back from Vancouver, Amanda cornered me...and, well, she told me what she knew and why she thought Kesley had died."

So they'd told Rafe what they'd told me in that cabin, and by the almost haunted look in his eyes, apparently I hadn't been the only one shocked by the discovery. Without realizing it, I had moved closer to him, wanting to seek some sort of comfort.

"I thought she was a good person," I whispered.

"I did too."

"Then what does that make us?"

"Fools, I suppose."

He had inched closer to me too. I could see the darker flecks of color in his irises, and only then did I notice how close we were to each other. My heart beat. Faster, faster. It was a strange and uncomfortable sensation I wasn't used to feeling around Rafe. Around any boy that wasn't Jackson, in fact. I saw his gaze flick down to my lips and then back to my eyes. For a few moments, I didn't move, and before I had a chance to, Rafe spoke. "Going to kiss me?"

I felt my cheeks flare at the audacity of his question. I rose to my feet, straightening my white, buttoned coat.

"You wish," I said with as much venom as I could muster.

A lazy grin. "And what if I do?"

I wasn't sure it was possible, but I swore my cheeks burned even hotter. He was watching me, waiting for my reaction, but I wouldn't give him the satisfaction of saying something idiotic, so I just turned and walked away.

"Ava, *wait*." I didn't stop, but my pace was nothing compared to Rafe's long stride. He caught up with me in no time. "I'm sorry. I am."

"Forget it," I said. "You were my sister's best friend anyway."

"So?"

"It would have been weird."

A hand on my arm made me halt, and I found myself staring directly at him.

"You want to know why I think you're still with Jackson after everything he's put you through?" His voice was rough. "I think you're *scared*. Jackson is everything you've ever known, and you're scared to move on." I felt my eyes fill with tears, felt my blood throb, because, *God*, Rafe was right, wasn't he? I was afraid of what would happen if there was no me and Jackson anymore. He was my safety net. My constant.

And I was scared that every day, another small piece of me was falling for Rafe. I desperately hoped I was wrong.

———

Lia finally spoke to me on Sunday.

She'd been avoiding every text and call since I'd blown her off at the coffee shop, and I didn't blame her. I had been cruel. Lia and I had been friends for as long as I could remember. Why had I been so horrible?

Early morning sunlight pushed through the cracks in my blinds, casting golden rays across the dust along the windowsill, when the shrill tone of the phone yanked me from my first peaceful sleep in a week.

"Can you get the phone, Ava?" I heard my mother yell from somewhere down the hall. I pushed the blankets off and speed-walked to catch the phone in time.

"Hey," I said a little breathlessly.

"Hey, Ava. You haven't been answering your cell." Lia's voice was stiffer than usual. Oh, right. Where had I even put the thing? I didn't remember. It had probably fallen underneath my bed.

"Look," I whispered as my mother's footsteps drew closer. I turned so my back would be to her. "I'm really sorry about what happened, but I'll explain."

There was a pause on the end of the line. "You promise? Swear on our friendship?"

I smiled. "Yes, Lia. I swear. When can I meet you?"

"Five minutes," she said, and her voice rose excitedly.

———

Circling Pines was a small town.

There was one high school, a gas station, one coffee shop, and a collection of clothing stores. Tourists occasionally passed through town, often on their way to visit the national parks, but other than that, Circling Pines was a place where most faces were familiar.

With her glossy, black hair, expensive leather

handbag, and red lipstick, Lia was the epitome of the upper class of Circling Pines. She could spend hours racking up charges on her parents' credit card, and as long as her grades remained high, they wouldn't blink an eye.

Needless to say, this wasn't me.

With my polka-dot skirts, turtleneck sweaters, and makeup so light you couldn't even see it, I clearly showed that fashion had never been my forte.

"What about this?" Lia asked twenty minutes after we'd arrived at one of the designer stores. She pulled a lacy, red dress from the rack with a flourish. "It's sexy."

I arched a brow, casting a glance over the silken material. "There's a fine line between sexy and slutty," I pointed out.

Lia's lower lip jutted out into a pout, but she shoved the red dress back onto the metal rack. She still trusted me enough to give her fashion advice, I realized, which was a step in the right direction.

"Shopping for someone special?" I asked as she continued to rifle through the clothes. Not that she needed any more. I'd seen her closet, and she had enough clothes to last a lifetime. It was funny how that worked; people always seemed to want more than what they had.

An intimate smile curved her lips, and she took her sweet time responding. "Maybe," she said.

"Who?" I asked, tilting my head curiously. While I had never really approved of the boys Lia chose to date, I wanted to know who had caught her eye this time. But Lia didn't answer, instead taking another dress from the rack. Pink and horribly frilly.

She held the dress up so I could see it better. "Thoughts?"

I scrunched up my nose. "Maybe if you were a five-year-old playing dress-up as a princess," I told her.

Something caught my eye through the mass of clothes, and I reached forward to pull out a black dress of respectable length. Lia snatched it from my grip, casting a well-practiced eye over the garment. "I like it," she finally said. Then she eyed me over the clothes rack, a gleam in her eyes reminding me why we hadn't spoken in days. "Look," she said with a sigh while fiddling with the price tag. "Should we, like, talk about what happened?"

I folded my arms across my chest. "I've been trying to contact you for two days, remember? You're the one who's been avoiding me."

"Whatever. I want to know now."

I sighed, closing my eyes briefly. What was I supposed

to tell her without dragging her into the mess of Kesley's death? I would have to give her a sliver of the truth, I knew, and I stared at her as she waited for me to say something. "They…" My throat seemed to close.

"They *what*, Ava? You know what they're capable of, and now you're suddenly best friends with them?"

"I'm not friends with them," I said. "They just wanted to *talk*."

"Then why couldn't *I* be there?" she asked, sounding a bit like a petulant child. She blinked a few times, as though she were holding back tears.

"They wanted to talk about Kesley," I said finally.

"Oh." A pause. And then, "What did they say?"

I fixed my gaze on the floor once more, avoiding her sharp eyes. Could I really lie to her face? Oh, they had told me something all right, but how was I supposed to explain that my boyfriend could be a *killer*? That was *not* the conversation for a clothing store. But looking at her, I could see she wasn't going to back down. I needed to give her something.

"Nothing much," I said. "They said that she was a great girl and that she shouldn't have died so young." That even sounded false coming from my lips.

"Oh please," Lia said, rolling her eyes. "And you think they're being genuine?"

I stared at her, uncertain. "I don't know, Lia. They sounded like it."

"Come on, Ava. They've sweet-talked their way out of so many punishments that I doubt *they* even know when they're being genuine anymore. They obviously want something from you."

She was right, as much as I didn't want to admit it. They *did* want something from me, but in this case, we both wanted the same thing. Did that mean we were using each other?

As I scrutinized the way Lia's mouth was pinched into a flat line and the muscles tight around her eyes, I was getting a pretty good idea what this was all about. Careful not to hit a nerve, I asked, "Is this even about me anymore?"

"What is that supposed to even mean?" Her eyes widened innocently.

I frowned. "Lia…"

Her eyes flashed. "So maybe you're right. Whatever, but you know what they did to me." She turned away, her expression concealed.

And so here we were: the real reason why I'd hurt her so much. A few months ago, Lia had fallen victim to one of their cruel pranks, and now I felt even worse about the situation—because what if Kesley had been involved?

Exams were a big deal for Lia's parents. They thought that doing well in school would set her up for a lifetime of success. This put the weight of the world on Lia, especially since her interests were centered on the latest gadget released. So she had struck a bargain with KARMA about her upcoming English test. They would give her answers to the test if she vouched for them as a witness at an upcoming hearing, which involved stealing ten cans of spray paint. She'd shown up and vouched for them—and KARMA had given her all the wrong answers.

On purpose.

That had been the last straw for Lia. Ever since then, her eyes turned cold at just the mention of their name. Not only had her phone and credit card been taken away from her, but her parents had filled her time with so much extra tutoring that I rarely got to see her except during school hours.

I focused on the present, on what Lia was now saying. I owed her that.

"I get it, Ava," she said. "I really do. Kesley was important to you. But it still stung."

I mumbled an apology, and everything fell back into its usual pattern until she said, "So what's with you and Jackson?"

I wrapped my arms around myself uncomfortably. "We're fine."

She cocked an eyebrow, her expression hardening. "That's all I get?"

Irritation poked its sharp claws at me. What was she expecting? Hell, what was I supposed to say? That I was beginning to fall for my sister's best friend and that I had no idea where that left me and Jackson?

"I don't know," I said, biting back a sigh. "He deserves a second chance, right? I think everyone does, even if they've done something terrible."

"Do you still love him?"

Her words caught me by surprise, and I found myself thinking about what Rafe had told me. If I thought about it, *really* thought about it, did I love Jackson? Truly? I felt different—stronger—around Rafe. But unpredictable too, and that scared me. Being with Jackson was safe. That I knew.

Was that really love?

I said nothing, and Lia gave me a look that was colder, less forgiving. In the end, I took too long to answer. "You don't even love him anymore, do you? He deserves *so* much better than you." And with that, Lia brushed past me without a backward glance. Leaving me alone again.

I stared after her, stunned, as she vanished down the street beyond, her words echoing in my head.

And I wondered: had that been *jealousy* in her voice?

I left the clothing store feeling empty.

Lia had always been...*Lia*. There for me but only some of the time—when it suited her, not me—and I had the persistent thought that if it came down to her happiness or mine, she would always choose hers.

I shook the thoughts from my mind. We were friends, right? We would get through this. In a couple days, things would go back to normal. They had to.

The gray clouds massing above me suggested rain or maybe, if I were unlucky, even snow. My feet crunched on fallen leaves as the shadows of four girls blocked my path, and I glanced up.

They were all there: Amanda, Riley, Abbey, and even May tagging along behind, hands in her pockets. She paused when she saw me, then made a beeline straight for me. I breathed out a frustrated sigh and repressed a groan.

"We don't have time for this," Amanda said in a bored voice when she noticed where May had gone, and her eyes flickered back and forth between May and me.

"We're going back to Riley's," May explained.

"You should come," Abbey said, a crooked smile curving her lips.

"Oh, hell no," Riley hissed, crossing her arms.

"Nah, give the girl a chance, won't you? Besides," Abbey continued, "there might be more Kesley in her than you think."

More Kesley in me? God, I hoped not. My stomach clenched.

Amanda's eyes glinted at that, sharp and beady like a hawk's. "Fine," she said, conceding, but her mouth remained set in that same flat, irritated line.

"What do you say?" asked Abbey, who was watching my expression carefully.

"Yes!" May jumped forward before I even had a chance to open my mouth and grabbed my arm, pulling me down the street.

Kesley would have hated this, I thought. *Hated this.* Others taking control of me, making decisions for me. I used to think it was because she wanted me to become more independent, less vulnerable, but now I knew it was because she liked the control. She'd gravitated toward the closest malleable thing in sight: me.

But as I walked alongside her best friends, I decided that tonight, she was no longer going to control me.

The sun had dyed the tops of the trees golden-orange as we followed the main road that curved around Circling Pines High and the cemetery and went deeper into the town's most heavily populated section. Most of the trees had been cut away for development there, and two-story brick houses obscured the faint outline of mountains.

Riley stopped at one of these houses, kicking open the rusty iron gate.

"Please tell me you have the key to the liquor cabinet," said Amanda as Riley unlocked the front door. Amanda yanked off her flats and threw them onto the polished floor. Flecks of dirt and mud splattered everywhere. The others followed suit, seemingly oblivious to the mess they were creating. I took off my own pair of faded pink flats but piled them to one side. Neatly. Away from the others.

I looked up to see Riley waggle her eyebrows at Amanda. "Of course I do. My parents leave the things I'm not supposed to touch in the shittiest hiding places." As if to prove her point, she reached over to the fake potted plant that sat on a carved, wooden table. She took a silver key out from under it.

"Where are they?" I asked. "Your parents, I mean."

Riley flashed a grin in my direction. "Away. On vacation somewhere."

"And they leave you here? Alone?" I asked skeptically.

Riley scoffed. "They don't trust me that much yet. Just 'cause I haven't been in juvie for a year doesn't give me free rein over the place. My brother's supposed to be 'looking after' me"—she bent her fingers into quotation marks—"but he lets me do what I want as long as I don't bother him."

I followed the girls into the living room, which was wide and spacious with a beamed roof. Everything looked so polished and so neat and so...not Riley. I wondered if her room was as neat and orderly as this, but I didn't ask.

She walked to a glass cabinet filled with gleaming bottles of alcohol. Nerves flipped in my stomach as Riley selected one, then flicked an amused glance in my direction.

"Scared?" she asked, a taunting lilt to her voice as she cocked an eyebrow.

My heart pounded. I was *not* an alcohol drinker. The feeling of not entirely being in control *did* scare me, but I wasn't going to tell Riley that.

Fearless, that manipulative, cold voice whispered at

the back of my mind. *You said you wanted to be fearless, Ava, didn't you? Then show yourself you are. Fearless.*

Riley tipped an even amount of liquor into plastic cups. I took the cup she offered me, my hands shaking. I saw her eyes flicker down to my fingers, and I know she noticed the shake, but at least she had the grace not to taunt me further.

I drew in a deep breath. Then I pressed the rim of the cup against my lips and tipped it back. The whiskey scalded my throat, burning down my esophagus, and settled uncomfortably in the pit of my stomach.

I coughed and spluttered, fighting the urge to retch it back up.

Amanda laughed.

There was the sound of someone hitting her on the shoulder, and May said, "Hey! Be easy on her! It's her first time with anything this strong."

This wasn't the time to tell her it was my first time with *anything*.

"What about Kesley?" I asked before I could stop myself, swirling the liquid around in my cup. I didn't look at the girls, not wanting to see their expressions. I wasn't sure why I had asked that—only, this was what Kesley did, right?

Get drunk, screw up, not give a damn?

"What about her?" May asked carefully, slowly weighing each word.

"I just wondered," I said with a shrug, "how often she'd do...*this*."

"Whenever things became too much for her," May said gently.

"Yeah," another voice said. Abbey? I didn't look up. "Remember the time Kesley gave you that vodka bottle? You puked all over my couch. The stains are still there too."

Oh God. Puking?

My stomach turned over further, and the back of my throat burned. "Can we not talk about puking?" I mumbled. Even the *smell* of this stuff made me feel ill.

Amanda smirked, seeing my discomfort. "How many cups d'ya think it'd take?"

"At least four," May said.

"No way!" Riley scoffed. "She's taken one gulp and she's already looking green."

"I'll bet my new sunglasses she won't make it through three," Amanda said.

"Yeah?" said May. "You're on."

I swallowed, stomach aching. *Fearless*, I thought over and over again like an incantation. *Fearless*. And no more Kesley. Not tonight.

Back at home that evening, I was looking for my
watch. I liked to keep track of time, because who knew
how much I had left?

A wink of gold caught my attention from across the
hall. And there lying right on top of the piano was
my watch. I stumbled over to it but didn't pick it up.
Instead, I pulled the stool out and sat down. I wasn't
drunk exactly, but I felt a certain lightness, a careless-
ness I wasn't used to.

I ran my fingers across the keys. Not hard enough
for them to make a sound but just enough to feel their
cool surface underneath my fingers. I sighed, closing
my eyes. For the first time in a long time, I wished *I*
had been the one to learn the piano. Music had never
come to me easily, and now I wished I'd tried harder.
I remembered bits and pieces, strung together in a
haphazard, messy way. I could partially play the right
hand on Beethoven's "Für Elise," though Kesley had
taught it to me quite a while ago. Still, my fingers
seemed to move of their own accord as, with my eyes
still closed, I felt along the ridges of the keys until I
found what I thought was the correct first key.

I pressed down. A quavering note hung in the air, high and sharp.

I breathed out a withheld breath and pressed the next note. I think it was right. At least it sounded right. I tried to imagine Kesley sitting there in the worn leather chair behind me, hands over mine as she showed me where to place them next.

Tears pricked my eyes, but I kept going. The melody was so painfully familiar that it made my heart ache, made every bone in my body wish Kesley were here with me to see this. Would she be proud of me now? Giving this a second go? My fingers moved up and down the keyboard, feeling the cool ivory. The melody and its keys were etched into my mind, and I was only half surprised to find I hadn't forgotten a thing.

I had to start over a few times—I'd missed notes here and there—but the melody sounded as smooth and haunting as I remembered it had for Kesley.

But then something sounded off as soon as I touched one of the keys. The pressure I had to apply was wrong, and the note sounded suppressed, as if something was trapped underneath.

The melody halted as I turned my attention to the key. My nails were long enough to reach under the key and pull it up slightly. Something white and flat caught the rays of dying light that streamed through the window.

I tugged it out.

It was a small, flat piece of cardboard, nothing more.

Red ink—at least, I hoped it was only ink—was splattered across the cardboard in a pattern that closely resembled blood. My stomach churned, but I forced myself to read the words written in large block writing in black pen.

HELP ME.

There were only two words, but they couldn't have had a more potent effect. My breathing seemed to shut off, and a ribbon of fear wrapped itself around my chest. I already knew Kesley's death was tangled up in something deeper, darker than I understood, but seeing this somehow made it much more real. Frighteningly so. It wasn't just the words she'd written, but the emotion that lurked just behind the ink. The fear, the panic, the hope all tied to two small words seen much too late. I swallowed down bile and tightened my already suffocating grip on the cardboard until it creased under the pressure. I couldn't be sure this note had anything to do with Kesley's killer. Maybe she'd just been depressed. Suicidal. Something other than what my mind had concluded.

And if this was indeed a plea for help, then why would she have hidden it away? What I couldn't grasp was why she hadn't told anybody about her fear. What was so terrible that she couldn't speak of it?

Everything felt wrong, like a puzzle that wasn't fitting together.

A rush of light-headedness washed over me. All of a sudden, it was too much, *all* too much. That, combined with the alcohol…

I think I passed out. I don't remember losing consciousness, but the next thing I knew, I was lying in a bed, and for one terrifying moment, I didn't know where I was. My eyes felt glued shut, and it took me a moment to peel them open. My head throbbed. Something cool was touching my forehead, and I jerked upright, the cloth on my forehead sliding off.

I rose to my feet and opened the door, and my mother, spotting me standing there, herded me back into my room.

"Lie down, sweetie," she said, pushing me gently by the shoulders until I fell back on the mattress. "You've been ill." I caught a glimpse of my pale-blue curtains and knew I was back in my room.

"What happened?" I whispered, my voice dry and scratchy.

"You passed out." My mother offered me a cup of water, which I took while watching her. She looked as though she had just come home from work, though the sky outside my window was dark. How much time had passed since I fainted? My mother touched my arm softly. "Were you playing the piano?"

I said, "What makes you think that?"

A knowing smile tugged at her mouth. "Apart from you being slumped across the keys, you mean?"

I grimaced. "Yeah, I was."

The realization of what had happened just before I passed out sank in slowly, and I bolted upright. I dug my hands into my pockets, searching for the cardboard I knew had to be there and ignoring the surprised look that crossed my mother's face. Explanations be damned at this point. I needed to find that note. But there was nothing in my pockets except wads of tissue and old gum wrappers.

"Ava?"

"Did you see a piece of cardboard? On the floor beside me? On the piano?"

"No… Is it something I should keep an eye out for?"

I blinked. "No, no, it's fine. Just some school notes. I can copy it from Lia tomorrow anyway. No big deal." But the words sounded flat even to my ears, and I wasn't sure my mother bought it. There was no way I wanted her to see what I had just found—not when *I* wasn't even sure what it was.

When my mother seemed satisfied I wasn't about to faint again, she left me to my own thoughts. After I was sure she was out of sight, I slipped from my bed and found myself standing before the piano once more. My gaze swept the floor. Nothing. Then the keys. Again, nothing. I ran my fingers through every nook and cranny of the piano. Not a single shred of the note remained.

Sighing, I turned and headed back up the stairs.

Part of me had always wondered what it felt like
to be bad. To do terrible things. To lie or steal or
break someone's heart. It must have felt good,
Kesley, if you did it so often. Was it a matter of
power? Were you tired of being that golden girl,
the girl everyone wanted to be? Maybe popular-
ity wasn't enough for you. Maybe being beautiful
still wasn't enough. Maybe having people around
you who loved and adored you grew tiresome and
boring. Maybe being that girl—neal, tidy blond
hair, fashionable clothes, commendable grades—
weighed you down like stones in your pocket.

I will probably never fully understand the things
you did or why you did them. Or if, even for a heartbeat, you regretted it all. Was there a tipping
point, a moment, where you'd just had enough?
When being the perfect daughter made you want
to scream and tear yourself from the inside out,
where the scales finally tipped from good to bad?

Was I part of that moment? Could I have stopped
that moment?

Sometimes, I felt cocooned by being good, by
being the sort of person people expected me to be,
not the sort of person I wanted to be.

What had that felt like, letting go?

What had that felt like, knowing that what you did and the things you said could break another human being? Look at what you've done to me. Are you proud, Kesley?

Sometimes, I hated you.

But other times, as much as I never wanted to admit it to myself, I wanted to be like you. Not the polished Kesley, not the sweet Kesley. The cruel one. The bad one. The one etched with shadow and hate, the one only a handful of people in Circling Pines had seen. Because sometimes, it was just so damn hard to be good. Being good could break a person from the inside out, even if everyone around them couldn't see.

And besides, Kesley, after everything, didn't I deserve to be a little bad...

CHAPTER

Nine

A FEW DAYS LATER, A KNOCK ON MY BEDROOM
door tore me away from studying.

Studying was a nice distraction. It made me think
of other things for once and pushed away some of the
lingering sadness. Math, at least, made sense. There
was a problem and a solution and nothing in between.

The door opened, and my mother appeared around
the corner. I could tell she'd just come from work; her
brown hair was twisted into the standard bun, though
now wisps of hair framed her thin face. It was gaunter
than a month ago, and the lines around her mouth and

eyes were more pronounced. She wasn't old, but for the first time since the funeral, I could see the weight of everything resting on her shoulders.

"What's up?" I asked, rolling some of the stress from my shoulders.

"There's someone here to see you," she said.

I grimaced. Only one person could elicit that sort of reaction from my mother. "Rafe?"

"*Yes*, Ava. What did I tell you about him?"

I tilted my chin up, defiant. "I know what you said, but he's a good guy. *Really*," I insisted when she raised her eyebrows. "Give him a chance."

Her eyes softened then. "Boys like that will bring you nothing but heartache." Maybe, but boys like Jackson hadn't brought me anything better.

So I said nothing to that, instead making my way downstairs after my mother and wondering what she'd think if she knew the full extent of what I felt.

I decided I probably didn't want to know.

Rafe sat at the table, dark hair unusually neat. I felt a rush of heat when I saw him there, so I looked quickly at my feet. I think he noticed though, because when I glanced back up at him, he was grinning.

Half a minute passed in uncomfortable silence while I fiddled with the blue ribbon weaving the hair away from my scarred cheek. Then, unable to take the ever-growing tension for a moment longer, I said, "I'm sixteen. I don't need parental supervision anymore. Rafe and I will be outside, okay?" My mother grudgingly agreed to let us go, so I grabbed Rafe by the upper arm and dragged him to the door.

"What were you thinking? Coming here?" I asked once we were outside.

A cold breeze whisked the reddish-brown leaves into a frenzy as we walked along the sidewalk, and my cheeks were freezing. From the corner of my eye, I saw Rafe shrug. He didn't answer my question but instead said, "What have you told your mother about Kesley?" Deflecting the question as usual.

"I haven't told her anything," I said. "Just because our ideas of Kesley have been shattered doesn't mean hers have to be." My voice was a little more than bitter, but what I said was essentially true. I had never considered Diana to be a strong woman emotionally, so how was I supposed to tell her that her daughter wasn't the person she thought she was?

Rafe cast me a sidelong look. "You don't think she deserves to know?"

Despite the icy weather, my blood heated. "Deserves to know *what*, Rafe? That her daughter lied and manipulated and stole? How am I supposed to tell her that? Sometimes, even *I* wish I didn't know."

He didn't say anything. He just shoved his hands into his pockets and said, "But you told her about Kesley and Jackson, yes?"

"Yes," I muttered, "but I'm not telling her about you-know-what. Kesley and Diana—my mother, I mean—weren't very close. Since Kesley was older than me when our real mother died, she has...*had*...never really gotten used to Diana. To her, Diana fostering us felt like an invasion, not an act of kindness. She doesn't need to know about KARMA."

"Fine," he said, his blue eyes intense, "but secrets have a way of coming to the surface eventually."

"Like bodies?" The words fell from my mouth before I could stop them. Rafe looked as though I'd slapped him. He didn't say anything, just stared at me. I was sure that shame was curling off me in visible waves; tears were pricking my eyes like needles. "I'm sorry. I don't know why I said that. It was..."

"Cruel? Harsh? Uncalled for?"

"Yeah," I said. "All that. But Rafe...I can't tell her any more. I just *can't*."

But for whose sake? Somewhere deep inside me, I

acknowledged that it would hurt me more to tell her what I'd learned.

I supposed that made me a selfish person.

I turned to Rafe, a thought occurring. "What do you think would have happened if Kesley had told someone she thought she was in danger?"

"I don't know," said Rafe, his voice raw with honesty.

I hardly heard his response. "Would it have made a difference? Would she be here today? I just don't..." My voice broke. "I just don't understand *why* she never told anyone anything."

"She had her reasons, her secrets."

"You keep *saying* that," I said, "but I'm no closer to finding out who killed her. She might've had her secrets, Rafe, but I'm worried that's what got her killed."

Frustration unraveled inside me. Frustration at Rafe's vague, ambiguous responses. Frustration that every time I thought I knew something, I really didn't.

A tense, coiled silence fell between us, and neither of us was willing to break it. We passed through the streets without a word to each other, with nothing but the whispers of cars on the highway and the crunch of frost and leaves underfoot. Only minutes later, we reached the park, where the late-afternoon sun gleamed silver off the playground equipment and the grass crunched with a fine layer of frost. I stared at the park without really seeing it. Here, Jackson had told me the truth, and weeks later, I was still asking myself whether I'd made the right decision.

Surely if I had, I wouldn't be second-guessing myself now.

I could almost feel Rafe looking at me. "You're thinking of him, aren't you?"

A moment of silence. I looked at the ground, where the ivy curled around a smaller, frailer plant, choking it. Ice clung tenaciously to both plants' leaves. "Yes," I said, breathing out a sigh, "I am."

"Do you want to talk about what happened the other day?"

I thought about the almost-kiss. Did I *want* to talk about that? No, I didn't.

I closed my eyes, suddenly grateful for the iciness of the wind. "Kesley?"

"Don't play dumb, Ava," Rafe said, his voice layered with the hint of a warning. "You know what I'm talking about—you and Jackson."

I opened my eyes, pulling my arms around myself self-consciously. "Then no," I said, "I don't want to talk about it." I tried to turn away, but a firm hand on my shoulder stopped me. I glanced up to see him staring at me. That might have been a mistake, because suddenly, I couldn't look away. Our gazes locked so tightly that I was sure nothing could pull me away from him. He took a step closer, and his hand gently touched my cheek—the roughened, scarred left one.

The one that Jackson could barely look at, let alone touch. A shiver of suppressed delight ran through me.

"Are you with the wrong boy, Ava?" he asked quietly.

I wanted to deny that. I wanted to proclaim him insane or at least arrogant for thinking so, but how could I do that when I didn't even know the answer to his question? A crooked smile curled across his mouth, like he knew exactly what was going on in my mind. The thought was disconcerting.

I jerked away, taking a few paces back. "You don't know what I'm thinking," I said fiercely. "God, you haven't changed one bit, have you? You still think you're irresistible. You still think you can flick a finger and girls will fall at your feet." The words exploded from my mouth in a bitter, hateful rush, and I stood there breathing hard, like I'd just run a marathon. Rafe's expression never changed, and for some reason, that just irritated me further.

He leaned forward, so close I could once again see

the darker flecks of blue in his eyes. "On the contrary, I've changed a lot. You just can't see it yet." He glanced up at the darkening sky. "It's getting late. You should go home."

He turned and started to leave.

"Oh, and Ava?" He twisted around, half a smile on his face. His blue eyes glinted. "You never *did* answer my question."

I said nothing. I just watched as Rafe's figure faded into the distance. I stood rooted to the spot until long after he had disappeared.

I was filled with a strange sort of emptiness as I walked back through the streets, feeling emotionally numb. It wasn't the aching emptiness of losing someone close to me but almost a detachment from reality as Rafe's words ricocheted like bullets in my head. *Are you with the wrong boy, Ava?* I wandered aimlessly for a time, unwilling to face home or, more accurately, my mother, who I knew would be watching me carefully.

I turned left onto my street, looking at the almost identical modern houses that lined the pavement. Time never changed things here, almost as if it had stopped entirely. Our garden was messy—weeds infested the neat rows of plants, and most of the flowers had died

long ago. Everything was covered in a thick coat of
frost too.

When I opened our door, the clang of pots and
pans told me my mother was cooking. I slipped quietly
past the kitchen and up the stairs to Kesley's bedroom.
I hadn't been inside since she died, but everything
looked frighteningly *normal*.

After her murder, the police had taken her phone
and laptop, but that had since been returned. The
room still smelled faintly of jasmine perfume, a cloying
scent that sent shards of sorrow straight into my chest.
I brushed the tears from my eyes with the pads of my
fingertips. Unable to stitch together enough courage
to take a step inside, I turned away.

Saturday, I waited for my mother to leave the house
before I went downstairs, knowing that if I didn't,
she'd want to talk. Still, when I came down, I found a
collection of emergency contact numbers scrawled on
a scrap of paper. A note lying beside it read, *Please stay
at home today. Love you. Off to run some errands.*

I didn't stay at home.

There were too many memories, too many

reminders, things that were just too hard to face alone in the empty house. So I tied my hair into a tight bun, brushed on a little makeup, and threw on the first set of clean clothes I could find. I headed out the door and into the crimson-and-gold-layered street. I had to check the door behind me twice to see if it was locked.

Diana would be back before nightfall, and I wasn't going to waste the precious little freedom I had by sitting at home, so I texted Jackson to say I was coming over. The day was cool and crisp, sharp with cold. I rounded the bend to his street, where the houses were larger, grander, with gardens that sprawled out graciously. His family's garden was neatly trimmed, nothing like the tangled mess that was our backyard. Neither my mother nor I had a talent for gardening, but the neat rows of hedges that lined the fence in front of me told a different story about the Palmers. A curved path cut through the garden and led to the front door.

The door was already cracked open when I got there. I pushed it wider and peeked into the house. A floorboard creaked somewhere. "Jackson?" I called to the empty space. There was no reply, so I steeled myself and headed up the staircase, walking past the family pictures and down the corridor to Jackson's room. His door was just slightly ajar, but that was enough.

A sliver of light fell across Jackson's bare chest, muscles rippling as he stepped forward, wrapping his arms around someone I couldn't see. I shifted my feet and saw the figure of a tall girl pressed up against the wall. I wouldn't have recognized her from the lacy undergarments she wore if she hadn't moved her head a particular way, her glossy, black hair falling like a sheet of black glass to expose her face.

Lia. Lia, Lia, Lia. *He deserves so much better than you*. Her words echoed in my head, a threat, a warning, a foreshadowing of *something* I should have seen coming a long time ago. But seeing them still hurt. It hurt so badly that I wanted to be sick. I felt a surge of emotion, fierce and hot, burning me from the inside out until my thoughts were disjointed. What I was seeing took a whole minute to reach my brain, and when it did, the burning, stinging sensation blazed into a roaring inferno. My head spun. The floors and walls were fading out, and I could focus on nothing but the images before me. My breathing became shallower, and every breath I took felt like it was filled with tiny needles puncturing my lungs. Maybe I had been sucked into a vacuum filled with nothing but the sound of my own shattering heart.

Thoughts blazed through my head, one after the other, entwining and changing so rapidly that it was hard to keep track of them. There was so much I wanted to do, so much I wanted to *say*, and the emotions raged through me like a hurricane. I could have stormed in there and wrenched them apart. I could have shoved her against the wall and punched her like I did Amanda. I could have done *something*—anything—that would extinguish the emotions burning into me.

I must have made some noise—a gasp or a yelp—because the two figures beyond the doorway halted. The soft sighs and moans were replaced with a deafening silence that grew and grew until I could barely stand it anymore.

I turned and bolted down the stairs.

I had just reached the door, the glorious sunlight at my fingertips, when Jackson called out from behind me. I heard his footsteps as he followed me downstairs.

"Wait, Ava, please…"

I spun around. "*Wait*? Wait for what? For you to spit more lies in my face?"

Jackson reached forward and touched my shoulder, but I jerked away so he couldn't touch me again.

"Don't touch me," I whispered, my voice clogged with emotion.

I turned. Took a step outside. Said, "You two make a cute couple."

And then I left.

I hardly noticed my way home. The streets flew by in a blur of tears and colors. The red blazing behind my eyes was either the color of the fall leaves or my anger. I couldn't tell. Didn't care either.

Maybe there was no difference. Everything was intertwined so intensely that I was surprised I found my house.

Before this, there have been only two moments in my life when I've felt betrayed. When my parents died and I was thrown into the foster care system. And when I discovered Kesley was not the sister I remembered, where I realized she was burying more secrets than I could have imagined. Now I could add Lia to that ever-growing list of betrayals.

My phone rang twice, three times, but I didn't pick it up.

The morning melted into afternoon, both of which I spent lying on my bed. My brain refused to be silenced, even just for a minute, and the tears that leaked from my eyes couldn't be stemmed.

Of course Jackson had gone for Lia. Who wouldn't?

It wasn't *her* sister who had been murdered; it wasn't *her* parents who had died; it wasn't *her* left cheek that was scarred beyond repair. She was the epitome of perfection, while I was filled with darkness.

There was a knock at the front door. Jackson? Maybe. I didn't answer, and after a while, whoever it was gave up and left me in peace.

I stumbled out of bed and made my way to the bathroom, bracing myself on the sink. The mirror took up most of the opposite wall. It was wide and vast, reflecting everything from the shower doors behind me to the windows, where white light was shimmering through the opaque panes of glass.

And there I was.

Just Ava.

Nothing special, nothing more than a girl with caramel-blond hair and mud-brown eyes. Lia could have been a runway model if she chose. She had the body. The hair. The long legs. But not me. Never me. I wiped a lone tear from my eye, staring blankly at my reflection. So what was to become of me in a few years? I'd fade from sight like a ghost, that person who was too afraid to step out of her sister's shadow.

I didn't want to be that person.

I didn't want to be one of those weak, fragile girls who tore themselves to pieces after a relationship ended badly. In the weeks since Kesley had died, everything had been taken away from me: my sister's memory, my boyfriend, and the girl who I thought was my friend. I didn't want to drown in sorrow. I didn't want to be powerless any longer. Because if karma truly existed, none of this would have happened.

It wasn't time to be sad anymore, to grieve. I was long past that. Anger began to coil tightly in my stomach like a rope. I clenched my hands along the curved edge of the basin, my knuckles turning white, my heart pounding, my head bowed.

And then…

"Ava?"

I looked up. Blue eyes stared back at me in the mirror, and I turned to face Rafe, even though I couldn't bring myself to say anything. I felt breathless, winded. I didn't need to say anything for him to realize something was wrong. "What happened?" he asked.

Absentmindedly, I touched my cheek. Tears still clung there, but my eyes were dry.

Finally, I spoke. "He cheated on me again, Rafe." There was a beat of silence. And then he pulled me into his arms, my cheek against his chest.

"I'm sorry," he said, his voice rough. "God, I'm so sorry."

I heard—*felt*—his heartbeat against my ear. What seemed to simultaneously be an eternity and no time at all passed us by. I said nothing, and he said nothing. Neither of us needed to.

I was the one to pull away and answer the question he was too careful to ask.

"Lia," I said softly. "It was Lia." His eyes closed briefly, but before he had the chance to say anything, I whispered, "How did you know I was home?"

"I didn't," he said, "not at first. But when you weren't answering any of my calls, I thought I should check on you." His gaze, strong and sure, held mine. A small but sad smile crossed his face. "And I'm glad I did. Actually, I came here to show you something."

Five minutes later, I found myself in front of the house and staring at the shiny black motorcycle Rafe was headed for. "No way," I said, stopping dead. Rafe shot an amused expression over his shoulder, and I could tell he was trying not to roll his eyes.

"Scared?" he asked.

"Well, yes."

He reached the death trap and unhooked an extra black helmet from it, throwing it in my direction.

I caught it. Barely.

"C'mon, you only live once, Ava. Besides, Kesley used to love it."

A hysterical sort of laughter escaped my lips. "No way! She would never have!"

"Oh yeah, she did. She liked the speed, you know? Said it was like flying."

I swallowed, a lump forming in my throat. If I closed my eyes and thought about it, I could almost picture it. I eyed the motorcycle hesitantly.

Seeing my discomfort, Rafe came closer. "Do you trust me?"

I sighed. "Despite everything, yeah. Yeah, I do."

I shut my eyes for a moment, then opened them. I'd told myself I would be *stronger*, less afraid of things, so this was a good step, right? I squared my shoulders and let Rafe help me tighten the strap appropriately and pull me onto the back of the motorcycle, trying very hard to not show I was shaking.

"Hold on tight," I heard him murmur before he revved the engine. Loudly. I pulled my arms around his waist, feeling the muscles there ripple as he switched the bike's gears. I pressed my face into his back, hoping he wouldn't notice as the tires screamed against the road.

I felt the wind rushing past me, tearing at my hair.

I literally had no idea where we were going. I refused to move my face from his back, so all I saw was darkness. I was terrified that if I moved an inch, I'd fall off the back. All I felt were the swerves of the bike. It was hard to tell, but he seemed to be driving up, up, up—the air growing colder around us—until he cut off the engine and blissful silence fell once more.

I drew in a deep breath. "We're here?"

"You're alive, aren't you?"

"Just," I said with a faint smile, pulling my cheek off his back.

I pulled off the helmet and glanced around, running my fingers through my hair, which was messy from the wind. I got off the bike. The mountains stretched out in the distance, capped with gleaming snow, and frost lay on the ground. A chain-link fence surrounded the edge of the lookout with a WARNING sign for the people who didn't see the impending cliff edge coming. A blanket of gold, brown, and green trees was spread out before me, covering the dip between the two mountains.

A valley.

My fingers itched to paint the scene before me. Picture-perfect. The dips and curves of the mountains, the challenge of mixing colors to find the perfect shades of gold and red for the sky. My stomach filled with ice as I thought of what had happened the last time I painted, and I pushed the idea from my mind.

A bench with green paint flaking off its surface rested in front of the view. I got off the motorcycle and walked toward the bench without thinking, gravel and frost crunching underfoot. Rafe joined me a moment later.

"Did you bring Kesley here?" I asked, knitting my fingers together for warmth. As much as I tried to avoid talking about her, I couldn't seem to help it. She was like a circle; she had no ending, and everything led right back to her.

"No," said Rafe softly, "I never did. We just…never seemed to have the time." This place seemed to have that effect on people, the desire to speak quietly, even though there was nobody in sight.

"Had the time?"

Rafe smiled ruefully. "She was a busy girl."

When I spoke, my voice was bitter. "Yeah. I guess living a double life doesn't give you much free time."

Rafe met my gaze, frowning. "She never lived a double life. She was just…" He trailed off.

"Just what?"

He sighed, shaking his head. "She was just Kesley," he said, as if that explained anything. And I guess in a way, that did mean something.

I just wasn't sure what yet.

Neither of us spoke for a few minutes, but that was one of the best things about Rafe. We didn't need to talk, to make meaningless chatter. It wasn't like with Lia, who talked and talked and talked without hardly breathing. For Lia, every silence was a moment wasted.

Lia. Her betrayal stung, and I couldn't seem to let it go, no matter how hard I tried to shake it off.

A warm hand touched my forearm, and I was brought out of my thoughts.

"Do you want to talk about it?" Rafe asked. His blue eyes were so sincere that seeing them made my heart ache. I looked at my intertwined hands, silent for a moment.

"I don't know," I said, sighing. "I guess so. I just don't know what there is to talk about. He's cheated on me. Twice now. Once with my sister, and another time with my best friend…" I trailed off, my mouth quirking into a humorless smile. "Maybe I just have bad taste in boys."

"Maybe you should consider that he's not the right guy for you," Rafe said.

"Yes, the thought *did* cross my mind," I said a little dryly.

Rafe laughed, then said, "I brought you here so you could get away from that for a bit. Maybe it's not forever, but it's still something."

"Thank you." Tears stung my eyes.

Rafe leaned his elbows on his knees, staring out across the view. His eyes were narrowed against the orange glare of the sun. "I never did tell you the whole story," he said moments later.

I stared blankly at him. "About what?"

"About why I never went to the funeral."

I shrugged. "You were upset. I told you that was okay, and I meant it." But I didn't look at him as I said it, instead staring toward the horizon where the canopy of golden trees melted into the sky. It was growing darker now, and faint pinpricks of light were becoming visible. Stars.

"I was in juvie again," he finally said.

This news didn't entirely surprise me. I bit back a sarcastic comment and instead said, "For what this time?"

Dying rays of light fell across Rafe's hair, highlighting the lighter parts with strands of gold. He refused to meet my eyes. "Kesley wanted a gun, so I got her one. And I got caught. That, combined with previous offenses..." He breathed out a sigh.

A cold, heavy *something* settled in the pit of my stomach. "A gun? You mean...because she said someone was after her?"

"I think so."

"*Please*, Rafe," I said, my voice edging on begging, "I know you think you can't trust me, but if you told me who she thought—"

"I don't know," he said, his jaw tightening. "And what makes you think I don't trust you?"

I sighed and leaned back. How many times had I gone over this in my head, hoping that some of it might suddenly become clearer? More times than I could count. I said, "I feel like...like Kesley couldn't trust me. Like I was this naive younger sister who wasn't old enough to understand anything important."

I felt his hand touch mine. "Ava, I would trust you with my life. I don't know why Kesley kept the things from you that she did. I really don't, but I also know that if I knew anything more about her death, I'd tell you." Rafe sighed and ran a hand through his hair, as if it wasn't mussed up enough from the wind on the ride up here. "Things are so screwed up, aren't they?"

I laughed. Yeah, that was one way of putting it.

I glanced up at Rafe, who was watching me with a faint smile.

My memory flickered back to that moment in the park when I'd been so close... I saw the blue of his eyes, the way his long eyelashes cast lines of shadow across his cheekbones. But I'd been with Jackson then. It had felt wrong, like I'd been the one doing something out of line. That was when it hit me: I was single now. There was no looming prospect of Jackson on the horizon, no point in fighting the feelings toward Rafe that scraped at my insides, longing to be out in the open.

I didn't realize I was inching closer to Rafe until I felt his breath caress my face.

We were touching now, his hand still resting on my forearm. Without thinking, without even considering the consequences, I curled my hand around the back of his neck and leaned in to him. I felt his hand snake around my waist, resting in the small of my back.

Just as my lips were about to touch his, Rafe murmured, "Wait, Ava..."

My eyes opened. When had I closed them? Rejection

crashed into me with the force of a truck, leaving me breathless. Tears sprung into my eyes, and I pulled away at once.

"Sorry," I whispered, my voice cracking. I let a curtain of hair fall across my shoulder so he couldn't see my expression or those stupid tears in my eyes. Maybe I had seriously misread the signs here. Maybe, once more, I had read too much into things. Tension curled thick in the air, and for a moment, neither of us said anything.

"Ava…"

"It's all right," I said finally, my voice oddly calm. "It's fine, I swear. If you don't feel the same, then it's fine."

"That's not what I meant," he said gently. "Not at all."

I breathed in the cold air, hardly noticing that the last rays of light were beginning to fade, the sky turning into streaks of navy blue and purple and red. He raised a hand to touch my face, and when I looked down, abashed, he tilted my chin upward, forcing me to look at him.

"You just found out your boyfriend cheated on you with your best friend."

"I don't need reminding of that," I muttered.

"My point is that you're confused."

"I'm not *confused*," I said firmly, determined to sound cold.

"You're confused," he repeated, "and you're angry. All you can think of is that your boyfriend cheated on you. If you want to kiss me another time, then I'm not going to stop you. Just not now." The sad smile remained, so soft I couldn't bear to look at him. He felt sorry for me. And I was so, *so* sick of people feeling sorry for me. I didn't want his pity.

Minutes passed in tense silence. When I looked back at Rafe and the embarrassment had cooled down to shame, I knew he had a point. He didn't want to kiss me like this. And if I were being honest with myself, I knew he was right. Completely right. I hadn't wanted to kiss him like I had that time in the woods. This time, something within me had felt different. A burning, jealous feeling had spurred me on. *That* wasn't me.

Rafe took my hand in his and pulled me to his side. He didn't speak, just let the silence we knew so well roll over us. I rested my head on his shoulder, staring out over the valley. Eventually, he would take me back down to Circling Pines, and I would have to face reality once more. Running away from my problems was pointless, even though every particle in me wished I could.

It was hard to recognize such beauty when I was so miserable. And yet, the glistening valley stretched out before us, the colors deepening, becoming hard to see. The sun dipped even lower, the stars becoming more defined, and I realized this peace wasn't going to last forever. Because I knew that even the most beautiful flower would wither and eventually die.

I sighed, barely audible, and we sat side by side like that for the rest of the evening.

It's hard to be bad if you care too much about the consequences. Every single decision we make holds a consequence. Like the night I tried to kiss Rafe. Looking back, I'm glad Rafe didn't let it happen then. Jackson's betrayal was too fresh for me to understand what that kiss would have meant.

The rest of that night was nice. Peaceful even. Although those days, "peaceful" was a relative term, because those dark, terrible memories were always lingering just below the surface.

You know, Kesley, I still remember the day they told us you were dead.

Dead. Gone. It was late afternoon, just as the sun was beginning its descent. Just before the policemen knocked at the door, I was the happiest girl in the world. Can you believe that? Just before my life came thundering down, I had actually been happy. That was all Jackson's doing, of course. Before things went so horribly downhill, everything seemed perfect. Pristine. He had been over that day, and the blossoming red flowers he'd given me sat in a vase on the table, catching the last rays of light streaming through the windows.

Then came the knock at the door.

At first, I didn't think much of it. It was just a

neighbor, maybe the old lady from across the road who wanted some company. But something didn't seem quite right. It wasn't a woman speaking. The voice was masculine, deep and full of sadness.

I remember standing at the end of the corridor, listening. Hushed tones and whispers. I couldn't see much, but the policeman's badge caught the light, winking at me as if beckoning me forward. And I remember this...feeling rising up inside me. I couldn't place it then, but I can now. Fear. My breath caught in my throat, and I grew light-headed. My heartbeat thrummed in my ears as all the blood rushed to my face. It's nothing, I told myself over and over again. It's nothing, it's nothing, it's nothing. But the last time I'd seen you was the previous night. When you didn't come back, we filed a missing persons report. The police had asked us where, if anywhere, you might have been. I looked up at the officer and said, voice trembling, "She loved Lake O'Hara. Maybe she's there."

I wish I'd been wrong.

And that was when our mother started to cry, and my breathing froze, and I realized it wasn't just "nothing." I think one of the policemen noticed

me standing motionless at the end of the corridor
because I remember him saying my name, though I
didn't know how he knew it. I never had a chance
to ask.

In his hand was a blue ribbon. Remember
that one?

But this time, it wasn't like I remembered. It
frayed at the edges, dirt covering its glossy layer.
It had been split in two, and it was curled and
stiff. As if it had been soaked through with water
and then left out in the sun to dry.

Everything after that turned into a blur of
emotion, colors, and sounds. It all blended so
seamlessly together over those past few weeks that
it was hard to tell each day apart. But I did remember the loneliness. The sitting in the dark every
night waiting, just waiting. I don't know what I
was waiting for; I knew you were dead. But some
part of me hoped they were wrong. That you would
stroll through the door any moment and proclaim
it all a joke.

You never did...

Ten

LIA AND JACKSON HAD NO PROBLEMS flaunting their newfound relationship at school on Monday. Hand in hand and displaying their relationship as if I hadn't been with him just a few days ago. Neither of them so much as looked at me, which I was fine with. Besides, I wasn't sure I could keep a strong handle on my anger, and I didn't want another Amanda incident. I'd managed to fly somewhat under the radar since then. Pitying looks were cast my way all day, and it was almost a relief to duck into the room designated for that afternoon's detention.

I didn't speak to Rafe that day.

I left school an hour later, and the sharp scent of cleaning agents assaulted my senses as soon as I stepped through my front door. The sound of my mother's soft crying came from the living room, and I knew it was going to be one of those days where it seemed that nothing would ever be okay again.

Diana never cried until Kesley died.

Even during the funeral, when I was racked with grief, she spent more time comforting me than crying. At night, she'd wait until she thought I was sleeping, and then I'd hear her crying through the walls.

Tonight was one of those nights where she just couldn't hold it in any longer. As I walked into the living room, it wasn't hard to guess why. "...Barely two months have passed since the tragic and brutal murder of Kesley Hale, and police still have no suspects. Kesley was an adored member of the community with a bright future ahead of her. Police are urging members of the public to report any suspicions sightings from that night."

I didn't want to listen to any more.

I reached over, found the remote, and flicked it off.

My mother looked up when silence fell. Her eyes were red and puffy, the lines of age more prominent tonight. I'd never thought of her as being old—she dyed her hair, which obscured most of the gray—but tonight, she just didn't look her age. She looked fed up, as if she wanted to crawl into bed and not get out for weeks. I knew that feeling all too well.

She wiped her eyes and took in a deep, shuddering breath, then smoothed back her hair like she did when she was nervous.

"Ava, sweetie, I didn't hear you come home. Do you want something to eat? There are some leftovers…" She trailed off. I just shook my head and sat beside her. She dropped her motherly facade when she realized it wasn't working on me. The tears that still streaked down her face were enough to tell me she needed me here. And I needed her.

"I just miss her, that's all," she said, her voice cracking.

"I know. I miss her too."

We were both silent for a moment. Then she said, "I was just thinking about Kesley and how she loved music."

My mother's eyes had taken on a faraway quality, the peacefulness marred by the sorrow that hung like mist in her eyes. "She used to play so much. Remember that? The house is so quiet now. Too quiet. Every day, the first thing she'd do after school, before even touching her homework, was practice her piano."

Despite everything, I felt a smile on my lips. It hurt, but it was a good sort of hurt. I wanted to cling to every memory of Kesley I could and guard them closely. I was so afraid that one day, when I was older, I would forget the small things about her. Like the jasmine scent of her perfume or the way her hair caught the light when she stepped in the sun. Or the way she used to play the piano.

"I remember," I said softly. "'Für Elise' especially."

"And 'Moonlight Sonata.' She loved that one too."

"She did," I agreed, at a loss for what else to say. We'd never really talked like this before. Not so openly, not so honestly. I stared at my hands.

The days had passed, and the sorrow held a tight grip on us. And when I did begin to realize this wasn't a dream, I had to find a way to deal with it. We both did.

I still didn't know how. How was I supposed to let go of someone, when once, my whole existence had revolved around her?

My mother sighed. "I still remember it, clear as day." She'd stopped crying now, but a pained expression twisted her lips into a grimace.

I was so deeply embedded in my own thoughts that my mother had to say my name twice to get my attention.

"Ava? Ava, honey, I saw Jackson today." My mother spoke softly, carefully. Like she was tiptoeing around a sleeping bear.

I blinked. "Oh. How is he?"

From the corner of my eyes, I saw my mother purse her lips. "He was with Lia. He looked…" She struggled for words. "Happy," she finally concluded.

"Good for him."

When I said nothing more, she asked, "Are you two…together anymore?"

I couldn't ignore a direct question, but I still kept my response short. "No."

"Why not?"

"Jackson has some issues with monogamy," I replied, averting my eyes. I didn't want her to see how much that still hurt me. The hurt wasn't just coming from Jackson but Lia too, and that just made things twice as bad.

My mother said nothing more on the subject of my personal life. Perhaps she'd sensed the stiffness radiating from me when she asked me those two simple questions. Perhaps she could see how much I still hurt from them. Instead, she asked me if I wanted some tea, and we spent the rest of the evening in silence. Finally, she said she had to get up early for work, and she left me for bed.

I stayed on the couch after that. I switched back on the television in a futile attempt to stop my somersaulting thoughts. I flicked aimlessly through the channels, feet curled underneath myself, until a news report caught my attention. An image of Circling Pines's mental health clinic took up most of the screen. It was a large, white building. Paint was crumbling from the walls, revealing the old, tired brick lying beneath. From the shot given, I could see sunlight gleaming off shattered glass littering the bushes below the windows. What was valuable enough in there to steal?

The reporter was saying, "Police have confirmed the mental health clinic was broken into last night and several patient documents stolen, but so far, no perpe-trators have been named. Eyewitnesses claim they saw three figures running from the scene, but this has yet to be confirmed by the police."

Why would someone steal patient documents? I narrowed my eyes at the screen as it flashed to a commercial, then just switched it off. Nothing, it seemed, could stem the flood of my thoughts tonight. I felt miserable but comforted myself with the thought that at least my night couldn't get any worse.

Of course, I was dead wrong.

The doorbell rang an hour after my mother disappeared upstairs.

I wasn't in any hurry to see who it was, but it rang one, twice, three times, so I slid off my seat and headed to the door, opening it a crack. Before I could pull the door open, someone pushed their way through and golden-brown curls filled the doorway for a moment. I stood there, stunned, before my feet propelled me forward, and I blocked her way. A strong smell of alcohol washed through the air.

Something had snapped inside Amanda. Her face was tear-stained, makeup running down her cheeks in black streaks, but she didn't seem to care. Pity curled around my heart as I watched her, unsure what to say. She'd been nothing but a bitch to me ever since I'd known her. Yet she had chosen to come here to me.

"Do—do you need something?" I whispered,

swallowing. She looked so vulnerable, so cracked, so broken. So much like…*me.*

"Can I stay here tonight?" she asked, surprising me.

I glanced up the stairway, the darkness telling me my mother was still sleeping. Amanda noticed my hesitant expression, and her eyes grew pleading.

"Okay," I relented. "Do you want some tea? Or coffee? I have coffee."

"Tea, thanks," she whispered.

I poured Amanda a cup of steaming water five minutes later. She sat at the table, staring at the marble countertop, though not really looking at it. Pain was etched into every feature on her face—from the sharp chin to the sunken eyes to the clenched jaw. I recognized that look. It was a look of hurting. She hadn't said anything, just let the tears run down her face in rivulets.

Is this about Kesley?

I chose a tea bag from the cupboard and dangled it in the hot water. Pushing it toward Amanda, I said, "Take it out whenever it's strong enough. I like it strong, but…" I trailed off, watching her. Her hands were lying on the table, and she looked lost.

"She did some awful things," said Amanda, "but she never deserved to die because of them."

"Kesley?"

A glint of familiar irritation crossed Amanda's features; it was almost a relief to see that. "Who else? Yes, I mean Kesley. I knew one of us would be really in deep shit for what we've done, but I never thought it would be *her*."

"Who did you think it was going to be?" I asked.

"Me," she said simply. There was no fear, no apprehension. She was only stating a fact. And this, I thought, was the first time I'd seen a glimpse past that facade Amanda thrust up for everyone to see. This was the first time I'd seen the true person. I wondered what May, Abbey, and Riley were all hiding beneath their facades.

Amanda raised a shaking hand to her lips, taking a sip of the scalding liquid. She averted her eyes from mine. Did she regret coming here? She put the cup down so it clattered loudly on the marble countertop. I cast a nervous glance toward the door, where the stairs were.

"Sorry," Amanda said, bitterness sharpening her voice. "Don't want your mother to see me here, do you?"

"Something like that," I murmured.

Amanda laughed, though there was no trace of

humor on her face. "You know what?" she told me. "You have it pretty good, Ava."

I couldn't stop my eyebrows from rising. "I have it good? Do you really think that having a dead sister who I barely understood is having it good? If the definition of 'good' has been changed to 'pretty shitty', then yeah, I guess I do have it good." My voice was harsher than I meant it to be. Amanda tipped back the cup and took a short drink of the tea. Her face wrinkled—I guess tea was an acquired taste—her eyes narrowing almost to slits.

There was a cold, tense silence.

Amanda toyed with one of the metal rings she wore on her middle finger. "You wanna know how I got mixed up in all this stuff?" she asked me. I nodded. She said, "You're okay here, aren't you? You have a nice foster family—"

"It used to be nice," I cut in flatly, "before my sister was murdered."

Amanda held up a hand. "Don't interrupt me, thanks. The vodka is going to fade any moment, and you're not gonna get another chance to hear this."

She was probably right about that, so I stemmed the flood of accusations that wanted to be heard. "Okay, sorry. Go on."

"I'm not so lucky. I *wish* I'd had a mother like yours. She would actually care if you didn't return home for days and came back stoned and drunk, wouldn't she?" When I didn't answer, she continued, "If you were to die, your mother would notice. I doubt mine would. Sometimes, she doesn't even remember my name. She was so drunk before she left tonight that she called me 'Miranda' until I corrected her, and even then she still looked at me like I was a stranger. Sometimes, I doubt whether she knows her left from her right."

"What happened?" I asked.

"My father happened," Amanda almost growled.

"I'm no stranger to parent issues," I promised her, and this was true.

"You are to ones like mine." Amanda fiddled with her hair, twirling it around and around her fingers. "He left my mother when I was about—oh, I don't know—thirteen. Sometime around then anyway. Only it wasn't like they had some massive fight. He just didn't come home from work one day. It was pretty scary, actually. He'd never done this before. Leave like that, I mean. My mother got worried, so she called the police and filed a missing person's report. And they contacted her the next day and said, 'You want the good news? He's alive. And the bad? He left you for another woman.'" Amanda spat on the countertop, her face twisting with anger.

I flinched and dropped my gaze, unwilling to look at her. "I'm sorry."

She laughed, but it was bitter. "You don't *need* to be sorry. I learned long ago that when people say that, they don't mean it. They say it because they feel like they have to."

I didn't say anything, because I understood perfectly what she meant. I thought back to the funeral and how all the apologies had begun to sound hollow after a while. "That still doesn't explain how you got on the wrong side of the law," I said.

"Oh, right." She paused, perhaps collecting her thoughts, and continued. "Well, life was pretty shit, like I said. Still is sometimes, but with the KARMA girls it's always much easier. That's why I joined." She paused to untangle a stubborn knot from her hair before she went on. "I didn't know Kesley that much before. She was just that pretty, perfect girl I walked past in the hallway, you know? The one who looked like she'd never touched a hair on anyone's head, the one who had boys drooling at her feet."

Yeah, I knew that girl.

Amanda continued, "But she found me crying

one day in the bathroom. She said she wanted to help me."

"Help you? How?"

"Have some fun. Break some rules. Get drunk. It wasn't supposed to be anything serious, but you know, a few times, we got close to getting caught."

"You were caught," I reminded her. "Heaps of times."

A smile curled at the corners of her mouth. "Oh, sweetie, you don't know the *half* of what we've done." And I suspected I didn't *want* to know either. "That was when it was just Kesley and me. It was cool then, but she suggested we should find more people like us. Who didn't give a damn about rules. Who just wanted to run wild for a bit."

I sank down low in my seat, pressing a hand to my forehead. "That doesn't sound like Kesley," I whispered. "She wasn't like that."

"Just 'cause someone never shows you a side of themselves doesn't mean it's not there. You have a habit of underestimating people, don't you?"

That stung. "What's that supposed to mean?"

She rolled her eyes. "Not all people are two-dimensional, you know. All you could see was the perfect boyfriend who wouldn't dare to cheat on you, right? Well, it's the same with Kesley. To you, she's the role model student who would do anything for her little sister. Maybe she wasn't. Maybe there was part of you that was always holding her back."

"I'd never—" I began hotly, but Amanda continued before I could finish.

"You don't remember your parents, do you?"

"No."

"But Kesley did, didn't she? She talked about them with me. Said she remembered every small detail about them. And guess what? It's not like she could have told you because *you* were too busy stewing in your own misery to even contemplate hers."

"That's not true," I whispered. "She could always talk to me."

Amanda laughed, a cold sound that reverberated off the ceiling. "Whatever. That's not the impression I got. Can't you see? She was just as cold and scared, as miserable as you were, and unlike you, she had no one to comfort her. So she turned to the only places she could: drugs, alcohol, violence. I guess that's why we were such a brilliantly matched pair," she added with a twisted smile.

"Yeah, well," I said heatedly. "It's not as much fun now that someone appears to be picking you all off, is it? Maybe she *did* deserve it after all. Who knows? You might be next." The words escaped before I could snatch them back. They hung in the air like poison.

Amanda's chair screamed against the tiles as she stood up, and I flinched at the thunderous edge to her gaze. She stood over me, eyes flashing, a snarl twisting her mouth. She grabbed my arms, holding me in a vice-like grip.

"Let go," I whimpered. "I didn't mean that."

"Whatever." She let go of my arm, leaving a red mark. "Just don't imply it was her fault for getting killed, all right, bitch?"

Meekly, I nodded, and then she settled back in her chair as though nothing out of the ordinary had happened. She continued her story, though I noticed the tight lines of tension around her mouth and eyes. She was still seething inside, I knew, so this time, I kept my mouth shut.

"We found the others next," she said. "May, Riley, Abbey. Kesley came up with the name. She said she wanted something that would stick, which KARMA did. We also liked the idea of people getting what they deserved. But that…that was when things began to go downhill."

"Downhill? How?"

"Kesley asked us to cover for her," Amanda said.

"Said she didn't want her reputation to be tarnished. She was right, I guess, because look where we are today, hey? None of us really wanted to do it, but we did anyway."

"Why?" I asked, my eyes narrowing. "If she was that awful to you, if she was asking you to take all the blame, then why would you?"

Amanda looked sideways at me. "Because she gave me something nobody else has, Ava. Belonging." She leaned her head against the cool marble surface of the countertop and closed her eyes. She looked tired; the lines around her mouth were softening out into smooth skin again. There was no more talk on the subject, though my mind still burned with curiosity and guilt. I couldn't deny that guilt. Its sharp edge grated at the thought of what Amanda had told me.

Why hadn't Kesley come to me? Talked to me?

Or even Diana?

But most of the time, it had just been us. Kesley and me. Diana's hours at work were crazy, but even so, I couldn't help but wonder why she'd kept everything to herself.

I stared out the window. A yellow glow highlighted the street beyond and the frost creeping across the lawn.

Something occurred to me then.

"Amanda," I said, and she looked up at the tone of my voice. "Why did you come here? I mean, don't you want to be with May or Riley or Abbey?" She glanced into the dregs of her tea. Her eyes narrowed as she scraped her wooden chair back. I cringed, thinking the sound would wake my mother.

"You're right," she said, flipping her golden-brown curls over her shoulder. "I probably shouldn't have come here. It's not like you're Kesley." She half sauntered, half stumbled out into the hallway.

"Amanda," I called out—but softly.

She turned with one foot out the door, her body angled toward me. Her eyes shone with unshed tears. "Whoever is responsible for this must be badly fucked up. Because Kesley *never* deserved this." With that, she slammed the door with a splintering crash.

I flinched and stood there, frozen, until I heard soft footfalls and spun around. "Who was that?" asked my mother. Her hair was pulled up tightly, her eyes still glazed with sleep, but her look of awareness told me she probably hadn't been fully asleep.

I shook my head, thinking quickly. "It wasn't anyone important. Just someone from across the street."

I stayed up for hours after that.

For the first time since I'd known her, Amanda had been open toward me. Gone for once was the girl who graffitied the walls and stole candy bars from the local corner store. Gone was the girl who made fun of me in the hallways, who stole answers for tests so she could pass. She'd become something more real to me.

Thoughts tumbled and twisted over each other until tiredness blurred them into an incoherent mess. I couldn't sleep. No matter what I thought of, I always ended up with the same unanswerable questions.

I sat on the edge of my bed and stared through the moonlit windows, running my fingers along the left side of my face absently. Tonight, my hair was pulled back, so why not be braver than usual? I slipped from the bed and entered the one place where I hadn't been since Kesley's death: her room.

The curtains had been pulled back and lamplight spilled through, illuminating the chestnut brown of Kesley's wardrobe. Shoulders back, chin high, I felt my way through the semidarkness and pulled the double doors wide open. The smell of mildew hit me first, and I recoiled, wrinkling my nose. Kesley kept most of her clothes in the chest of drawers beside her bed, leaving the wardrobe for old clothes she thought weren't cool enough to wear to school. A few long bags from the dry cleaners hung down, encasing long gowns she wore to school dances.

I felt through them, not searching for anything in particular, more letting the feeling of nostalgia wash over me. My fingers scratched against the hardwood back of the wardrobe. Struck by sudden inspiration, I ran my fingertips along the edge of the wood, searching, searching, until I found a slight groove.

If you weren't looking for it, you'd never know it was there.

Kesley liked to hide things. Underneath piano keys, behind paintings, underneath loose floorboards, and wherever else there was a slip of space. So why not here? I slotted my nails into the small grooves in the wood that ran around the back of the wardrobe and pulled forward. There was a grating sound, a squeal that made the hairs on the back of my neck stand at attention, and the plank of wood fell out of place.

I stared at what lay behind the plank. Highlighted by the thin beams of lamplight lay rope.

Rope?

I yanked it forward until it fell loose, and soon, a weathered and knotted piece of old rope was curled in my fingers. The piece of rope was brittle and old and felt like it might snap if I held it too tightly.

Rope. Kesley had *rope* in her wardrobe.

But that didn't unnerve me as much as the way the rope was twisted to form the shape of a circle.

It looked like a noose, and the sick irony of it all was not lost on me.

I stuffed it back into the wardrobe and slammed it shut, not even caring if my mother came to investigate what the noise was. I couldn't breathe, knowing what I'd just seen. My heart pounded, my hands shook, my stomach rolled. Had things really gotten that bad? Had things descended to that point where Kesley would have…?

No, surely not.

I stumbled back to bed in a daze, closing the door quietly behind me. I didn't know what to do. I crawled into bed and covered my head with my pillow, letting salty tears soak into it. If I had thought going into Kesley's room would give me comfort, I had been horribly wrong.

I closed my eyes. I didn't intend to drift off, but I must have.

At first, the only thing I noticed was the darkness. A suffocating, thick darkness. Slowly, carefully, someone placed the scratchy tightness of a rope around my neck. It was no longer just the darkness that felt suffocating. I clawed at the rope around my neck, my nails splintering with the effort. My heart pounded in my chest. Warm blood oozed over my fingers, and the more I tried to breathe, the more I tried to *survive*, the tighter the rope became. I stretched my mouth into a scream, but all that came out was a sort of strangled gurgle. Panic flooded me. Hot and cold. Sweat dripped down my shoulder blades. And amid the panic, the all-consuming fear, I wondered: *Am I going to die?*

I jolted awake, a silent scream curving my mouth. I sucked in breath after breath, my throat spasming. Cold sweat made my clothes cling uncomfortably to my skin. *A dream*, I thought, curling my hands around my neck and feeling the roughened, warped skin. *It was just a dream. Dreams can't hurt me.* But that knowledge only made my stomach tighten with illness. For me, of course, it had only been a dream, but for Kesley...

Was this what it had been like? A breathless despair,

a clawing, terrible desperation? Did she claw at her
attacker? Did she fight for her life?

I breathed out a shaky, controlled breath.

I rolled over in my bed and twisted the pillow
underneath me, closed my eyes, and prayed for dream-
less sleep.

CHAPTER

Eleven

ON TUESDAY, AMANDA DECIDED WE WERE
going to do something about Kesley's murderer.
Chilled morning air hit my face as I made my way to
the park where we had agreed to meet. Partly because
it would be empty early in the morning and partly
because none of us wanted to talk about everything
at school, where we could easily be overheard. What if
the killer was at our school?

Since I'd found that rope in Kesley's wardrobe, my
dreams had been filled with lakes and blood and frayed
ropes, and sleep was scarce. So when light started

creeping over the horizon, I'd called it quits and gotten up. The town of Circling Pines was still shrouded in a thick jacket of darkness, and as I walked with Rafe down the street, a shiver went through me—and not because of the cold.

The thought that this place, my home, was no longer safe made me shake.

Riley had a sour look twisting her face as I neared her. She was leaning against one of the street lamps, her cropped red hair gilded with gold from its shine. May lurked in the shadows just behind Riley. Abbey was beside Riley, headphones stuck in her ears as usual. When she saw Rafe and me approaching, she pulled them out and gave us a wide smile.

"Is Amanda here yet?" I asked once we were within hearing range.

Rafe and I came to a stop on the path that led into the trees. They looked dark, more menacing than usual.

Riley flicked a glance at Rafe. "What's he doing here?"

I stared at her coolly. "I brought him along. So Amanda isn't here?"

Creases appeared around Riley's mouth, making her look as though she wanted to say more about Rafe. But she only said, "Not yet. She'll be here when she is."

Despite our conversation last night, I wasn't surprised Amanda hadn't shown. And not just because she'd have a killer hangover right now. She had been more honest with me last night than anyone had been in a long, long time.

Silence wrapped around us, a tense, cold silence. I was the first to break it. "I want to go to the police," I said.

"Oh yeah?" Riley's voice was taunting. "And tell them what?"

"*Everything!* Riley, everything we could tell them might help—"

"Kesley didn't want their help," said Riley.

"Why?" My eyes stung with angry tears. "Because it might ruin her perfect reputation? And why does any of that really matter anymore? She's *dead*."

"Standing here arguing about it isn't gonna do Kesley any help," said a voice from behind us. Amanda had shown up. I turned around, hoping to catch her eye, but she avoided my gaze. She stood just outside the lamplight, which cast her face in deep shadow. Not that I really expected anything more from Amanda, but I couldn't help but feel a stab of disappointment that she wasn't showing me the open side of her that I knew she could.

"This was all your idea," I reminded Amanda harshly.

"Yeah. And I came here to actually *do* something. Not just come up with stupid ideas that aren't going to get us anywhere."

"You know what normal people do when someone is murdered?" I said. "They let the police deal with it. So what are we doing here exactly?"

"We're gonna do something about it. Either you're in or you're out, Ava. The choice is yours."

But, really, she was not giving me a choice, and we both knew this. "Fine," I said through clenched teeth. "What is it that you want to do?"

"We go back to where it all started," she said.

"All started?" I echoed, confused. "What do you mean by that?"

"Lake O'Hara," said Riley. I focused my gaze on her, unsure of what she meant. When she saw my expression, she said, "You used to go there every summer, right?"

"Yes, of course. But—"

"But *what?*" spat Riley.

"What good would that do? The place was searched by the police, Riley. It was cordoned off for *weeks*, and I'm no detective."

"I think Ava is right," Rafe said.

Her narrowed eyes snapped to him. "What other choice do we have?"

"How about we just let the police figure this out? *Please*, Riley," I said.

Going back to the lake wasn't appealing in the slightest. It would dredge up memories and emotions I would much rather forget. *I am like glass*, I couldn't help but think. Those memories would be the ones to make me shatter. I just knew it. Going back there without Kesley would hurt too much.

Rafe was watching me knowingly.

But my opinions were outweighed. Amanda stayed oddly quiet, looking at me every few moments, but May and Riley seemed to be resolutely set on the idea of going to Lake O'Hara. Even Abbey just shrugged at me when I cast her a final pleading look.

"We need time, Riley, and we don't have that. We'd need to stay there at least overnight if we wanted to find anything substantial, and bookings have to be done months in advance." It was a weak excuse, and we all knew it.

Riley said, "It's almost freakin' winter. Who's going to be there now? And we don't have to take the shuttle bus or anything. We can take the access road."

There were two ways to get to Lake O'Hara: either

hike down the eight-mile access road or take the shuttle bus. In the summer, the shuttle bus was always packed with tourists, so we would hike down the path. The hike was bearable, if not a little bland, yet hiking down a gravel pathway for two hours didn't sound like much fun with the impending winter.

This isn't about fun, I reminded myself. *This is about catching a killer.*

And besides, Riley had a point. Not many people would be there now. Tourists were generally scared off by the cold weather, and with Kesley's murder, Lake O'Hara wasn't where most people wanted to be right now. It would be the perfect time to sniff around.

I felt a flutter of brief panic, sensing that this conversation was rapidly drawing to a close. I wanted to put up a stronger fight, but what would make these girls change their minds? I was scared, plain and simple, and I knew that wasn't going to be enough of a reason—for Riley and Amanda especially. May would be a touch more considerate, and Abbey seemed indifferent to the whole situation.

And sometimes...sometimes, I fought so hard for things that I forgot what I was fighting for. *Kesley*, I had to keep reminding myself. I was fighting for Kesley.

"Fine," I said.

"Ava..." I looked around at Rafe, who brushed his fingertips along my cheekbones. "You don't have to do this."

"I do," I said. "For Kesley."

I searched his eyes, begging for him to understand. Eventually, he just sighed, and I knew that was the best I was going to get.

I turned to Riley and the others. "When are we leaving?" I asked.

Riley's mouth curved in a triumphant smile.

The sun rose over the next half hour, sending chinks of golden light across the tops of the trees as we worked out the details. We were to leave this Friday and return Sunday afternoon, which should give us plenty of time to find *something*. I remained adamant that we'd find nothing, but there was a dangerous gleam in Riley's eyes that told me not to argue.

The next part proved more difficult. What on earth was I supposed to tell my mother? For the others, it was easy. But, of course, they didn't have a mother who watched them like a hawk.

"Lia?" May suggested. "Say you're sleeping over at her house for the weekend. Studying for a test."

I raised an eyebrow at her. "That's not going to work," I said.

"Oh." May shrank back into the receding shadows, realizing what she'd said. "No, of course not. Sorry."

"I'll figure something out," I said to Amanda and Riley, who just nodded, not offering any advice.

May pulled me aside as the others began to move away. Amanda was already halfway down the street, Riley close behind. Abbey gave me a halfhearted wave before following the rest of her gang.

"Sorry about Jackson," May said bluntly. "I didn't know what he was doing. Honestly. I'd have told you otherwise." I looked at the brown hair that fell just past her shoulders, the open-faced expression, the way her eyes looked almost exactly like Jackson's. I felt my lips rise into a reluctant smile. I'd always thought of May as the cruel one, but oh how wrong I had been.

"I didn't think you knew," I said. "And you don't have a reason to be sorry."

She grimaced, looking over her shoulder at the rest of her gang. She said, "Thanks, Ava. I'll see you at school." I watched the four of them disappear down the street and around the bend.

"Amanda seemed quiet," Rafe said from behind me.

"Yeah." I glanced up.

"Want to explain why?"

I found it slightly hypocritical that he expected me to tell him everything when he was carrying more secrets than I could possibly imagine. Still, I explained what had happened with Amanda at my house the night before. He listened, not interrupting until I finished my story and explained my fears about everything, even what Amanda told me.

And still I was careful not to mention the rope. He didn't need to know about that.

Rafe's voice was gentle, careful, when he spoke. "It wasn't your fault," he said. "Whatever Amanda said, it still wasn't your fault. Kesley made her own decisions, and you made yours."

My eyes stung with unshed tears, but I didn't let them fall. "But I could have said something, Rafe. I could have *done something*, and maybe she wouldn't have hated me so much—"

"She didn't hate you," Rafe said so quietly I wasn't sure I'd heard him correctly.

"It sure felt that way."

He cupped my cheeks with both his hands, looking me in the eyes. "I'm sure you knew your sister better than I did, but if there's absolutely one thing in this world I am sure of, it's that she loved you."

He was wrong. I wasn't sure I really knew her at all.

I didn't say anything more and instead let him take my hand and lead me through the park. Early morning light peeked through the tops of the trees not long before school was due to start. The park was almost empty, with just a few early morning walkers enjoying the serene atmosphere.

Rafe pulled me into the trees and up the winding path that led to that place he'd taken me once before, the place where I'd almost kissed him. I felt my ears and cheeks redden at the thought, and I turned away so he wouldn't be able to see me blush.

We rounded a bend and there they were. Wrapped around each other like they didn't know when they'd see each other next. Lia's hair gleamed in the sunshine. They were entwined on the same rock where I'd perched only a few weeks ago. Rafe coughed loudly. They broke apart and glanced around, Jackson's arm still slung around Lia's slender waist.

"Yeah?" It was Jackson who spoke, his gaze darting back and forth between Rafe and me, and then I noticed how our hands were joined together. I pulled away, wrapping my arms around my middle. "You got a problem?"

"It's okay," Lia said finally as she pulled herself from Jackson's tight, almost possessive grip. She moved, her steps lithe and sure, until she stood before me. She slanted her gaze at Rafe, who got the hint and strode to the edge of the tree line, hands in his pockets.

I stared at Lia. She was looking away from me, over my shoulder, and the awkwardness was almost palpable.

"Hi," I said.

"Hey," she said. "So, we haven't talked since—"

"Since I saw you kissing my boyfriend. I know."

She sighed, steam gushing from her mouth. Her eyebrows narrowed, and she tucked her hands into her pockets, obviously uncomfortable. "I like him, Ava. I really do. I..." She trailed off, then met my gaze, her eyes as hard as steel.

I will not cry, I will not cry, I will not cry. I repeated the mantra in my head, hoping that if I said it enough times, it would become true.

"That's not *fair*, Lia," I whispered, my voice almost a hiss. "You and Jackson were the only people in my life that I felt like I could *trust*. And you...you took my friendship and you tore it up like it meant *nothing* to you."

A flicker of something—maybe sadness, maybe regret—passed over her face. "I'm sorry, Ava. I... It was never, ever supposed to happen like this, I swear. I thought that after that last time, you would have ended things. You would have gotten over him, and everything would have been fine. And when you didn't..." She swallowed, rocking back on her heels, then said very quietly, "Do you think we can still be friends?"

Could we? Could we go back to that place after everything that had happened? *No.* There was no doubt, none at all, that everything had gone too far for that to happen. I didn't have to say anything to Lia.

She saw the answer already written on my face.

She turned and walked away, stalking back to Jackson and tugging him along the trail to the main road. I watched her, but she didn't look back at me, and I felt a sharp sting of...what? Not jealousy really. More sadness for a friendship I wasn't sure could ever be repaired.

I breathed out a sigh, turning away.

Rafe was watching Jackson leave with narrowed eyes, a twitch in his jaw. When he saw me watching him, he said, "Just say the word and I'll punch him till he's black and blue."

I rolled my eyes. "While I find your show of protective manliness flattering, he's not worth it."

Rafe regarded my expression for a moment. "You don't look upset," he said, his eyebrows lifting slightly.

I shrugged, wrapping my arms around myself. "I don't miss him as much as I thought I would. I think my heart was already fractured before he broke it completely." For the first time in a long time, perhaps longer than I'd first realized, I didn't feel overwhelmed. I wasn't sure why this was. After all the things that had happened, shouldn't I have been feeling worse? But there was something about being with Rafe that seemed to lift all the worries from my shoulders or at least ease them a bit. I felt their presence lurking in the back of my mind, but I could push them back, allowing my mind to focus on other things.

A comfortable silence fell, and Rafe cast me a sidelong glance. "You know," he said, "the last time we were here, you tried to kiss me." A teasing smile played around the corners of his mouth.

"Oh" was my ingenious response. I looked at my interlocked fingers. He touched my arm, an indication he wanted me to look up at him. But that would be a mistake, I told myself. A mistake I would never be able to come back from. Still, the lingering warmth of his hand on my arm made me lift my head. And so I did the only thing that felt right at that moment: I kissed him.

At first, it was nothing but a soft brush of our lips. I wasn't sure whether I intended it to be anything more than that. I wasn't even sure Rafe wanted more than that. But kissing Rafe was different from kissing Jackson. With Jackson it had felt normal, routine almost, just like getting out of bed and brushing my teeth was.

This was different—wonderfully, surprisingly different. Before I could tell what was happening, Rafe had pulled me to the ground, and my back was pressed against the springy grass. His fingers traced trails of heat up and down my arms in mesmerizing patterns, drawing a sigh of content from me. I wrapped my arms around his neck, pulling him closer until every part of our bodies touched.

My body relaxed into his as the butterflies I'd been feeling just moments before faded, until there were just the two of us, his soft lips caressing my own, tasting of mint gum that barely disguised the bitter taste of cigarettes.

A moment later, I drew back, breathing in a lungful of air.

He kept his arms around me, almost protective,

and watched me. He did that a lot—watching me. Examining my expression, seeming to dissect every emotion that passed over my face. At that moment, I didn't care because I was here with Rafe, and although it had taken me a long time to get to this point, this was something I'd wanted for longer than I really knew. With his lips still brushing mine, he whispered, "Ava…I'm sorry. I shouldn't have—"

"Don't," I whispered, curling my hand around the collar of his shirt. "Please…don't. For the first time since Kesley died, I feel alive."

That seemed to be all the encouragement he needed. Rafe groaned and pulled me closer until every part of us touched. His hand snuck underneath my shirt, tracing intricate patterns on the skin there, making me sigh and arch closer. His fingers teased the edge of my bra but went no farther than a brush of his hands across my breasts.

"That was unexpected," he murmured, lips still close to mine. I flickered my eyes up to his and saw that they were crinkled into a smile. "What do you think Kesley would have thought about that?" I brought my hand up to touch his face, warm under my fingers, rough with stubble.

"I don't know," I answered honestly.

And it was strange she wasn't here anymore to dictate who I dated. I remembered in eighth grade when Lia told me Thom Gate had a crush on me, and Kesley said I couldn't date him. She'd had this steely look in her eyes, a warning that was only second to our mother's. But like the stubborn eighth grader I had been, I'd gone out on a movie date with him anyway. I realized she was right when afterward he'd tried to stick his hands down my pants. I'd come home crying. That was one of the things that irked me so much about Kesley—she was often right.

I thought back to Lia and Jackson and remembered how my mother had commented on how happy she thought he looked—

Lia.

That elusive thought that had slipped through me for the past few days clicked into place. I snapped up into a sitting position with dizzying speed, closing my eyes as the world spun around me, as the blood rushed back up to my face all at once. It had only been when I thought of Kesley and Lia at the same time that it made sense. A cold feeling sunk through my skin, chilling me to my core.

"Ava?" Rafe's hand was suddenly at my shoulder, his lips at my ear.

When I spoke, my voice was calm and measured.

"KARMA pulled a stunt on Lia not that long before Kesley died. Rafe, what if—" My breathing became jagged and sharp, and I couldn't even finish the sentence. The thought that Lia could have done something like that...

But why not?

Rafe was silent for a moment. Birds chirped above in the trees, but everything apart from Rafe and my mind seemed far away, as if I'd been transported into an alternate universe, somewhere where my worst night-mares seemed to be coming true at an alarming rate.

Desperately, I tried to reason. Of course, it couldn't be Lia—that was impossible. Lia was Lia. Obnoxious, selfish, but not a killer. *Right?* Then I thought of the way she'd been oddly silent during the weeks after the incident had happened—and then, miraculously, just after Kesley had died, she'd gone back to normal. She'd seemed happier somehow. Was it because my sister was dead?

"Did Lia somehow found out about Kesley's involvement in KARMA?" I said. A shiver ran down my spine.

"I think you're overreacting," Rafe said slowly. "How would she even know about Kesley and KARMA?"

I swallowed. "Lia can be persuasive. She might have asked around. Kesley couldn't have kept *every* tiny detail hidden."

Rafe still seemed unconvinced. He placed a hand on the small of my back, and I liked the warm weight there. It made me feel protected. Still, I couldn't ignore the fluttering of fear in my stomach. It was the same feeling as with Jackson: the fear that someone so close to me could have done something so cold-blooded. Would it have been worth it? Were fake test results worth getting her hands so dirty with blood? Would Lia have descended to such a low—all for a little payback? And Rafe was right. I had no answers to any of the questions that swirled around in my head, seemingly endlessly.

Rafe moved his hand from the small of my back to wrap around my waist.

"I'm afraid," I whispered, turning in to him.

"I know, I know. But nothing is going to hurt you while I'm here, okay?"

"Promise?"

His arms tightened around me. "I promise."

I woke that night to my door creaking open.

Moonlight filtered through the thin curtains, sending a ribbon of silver light falling across the carpet and to the door, where a pair of feet stood. I recognized the fluffy, pink slippers. I yanked myself up in bed, heart slamming into my rib cage. Icy fear slithered through my veins as I shook the last remnants of sleep from my eyes, preparing for the worse.

"What happened?" I said, my voice dry.

No reply. The door just creaked open farther, revealing my mother's slender figure against the bright-yellow light issuing from the hall. She said nothing for a brief moment, but as she tilted her head slightly, the moonlight washed over her face. My stomach swooped; mascara ran down her cheeks like she'd been crying, and her eyes were red-rimmed and swollen.

I sat up straighter. "Are you okay? Mom, what happened?"

"Sorry, sweetie," she said, almost whispering. She sounded strained. "I didn't mean to scare you." And that was when my mother laughed: a shaky laugh, but a laugh nonetheless. She hadn't laughed since before the funeral.

"Nothing's wrong, Ava, nothing at all. Someone's been arrested for Kesley's murder."

Suddenly, I was wide awake. "W-who?" I could barely choke the words out.

"That girl…Riley Stone."

For a moment, I couldn't breathe. Couldn't think. The world closed up around me, and all I could see was darkness. The police wouldn't make an arrest like that without damning evidence, would they? An image of Riley this morning crossed my mind. Looking at her, it wasn't hard to believe she was the killer.

"Ava? Ava, did you hear what I said?"

"Yeah, I'm just… I mean, that's great!" I felt ill just thinking those words, let alone saying them. Once my mother had left, I sank back into my pillow, wide-eyed. Could Riley have killed my sister? I hadn't known Riley very well. But like Amanda, she seemed fiercely loyal to Kesley, so why would she kill her?

Everything changes after a tragedy. From the way you look at life to the way you act and the things you say and do.

Since you died, Kesley, I'm not the only one who's changed.

Your closest friends—Amanda, Riley, Abbey, May—would have remained on the outskirts of my life as girls I couldn't, wouldn't understand. I'm not saying we became friends—I don't think I could ever be friends with them—but neither are who I thought they were. They aren't just girls who liked to break rules.

They were loyal to you. They loved you, Kesley.

They cared about what happened to you and are determined to uncover the truth. If you hadn't died, what would my life be like? Where would Rafe and I be? Would I still be with Jackson, unable to see that what we had wasn't what I truly wanted?

And although it's a terrible idea to entertain, good things sometimes come from tragedies, don't they...

Twelve

PEOPLE WERE STARING AT US.

And by us, I meant me, Rafe, May, Abbey, and Amanda—a group of people I never would have thought I'd be sitting at a lunch table with, but I was. Last night's news hadn't given us a choice.

A buzz escalated around the cafeteria where everyone ate their lunches. People seemed to feel safe now that Riley Stone was in custody. The tension that had pressed down on Circling Pines had eased, though the four people sitting around me were feeling the exact opposite.

Only scarce details had been released about Riley's arrest, but it was still all over the news this morning. I'd switched on the TV the moment I got up, and my mother and I had sat on the couch, steaming mugs of coffee clutched in our hands. No matter which channel I switched to, Riley's face was there—twisted smirk, cropped red hair, and narrowed eyes.

This is all over, I told myself. *Riley is the killer. My sister's murderer has been caught.*

Yet I still felt a flicker of uncertainty. And the more I thought about it, the more I doubted she was the killer.

The police had been granted a warrant to search her house for drugs but instead found a piece of rope smeared with blood under a loose floorboard.

But something wasn't adding up. Surely if Riley had murdered my sister, she wouldn't have left evidence underneath a floorboard. Wouldn't it have made more sense to burn it, bury it, or throw it in the lake? Why hide it underneath the floorboards?

No, everything seemed too perfect, too orchestrated.

Our table had been quiet for the past few minutes. I don't think any of us knew what to say. We were such a mismatched group that none of us had much in

common, apart from Kesley. We were all linked to her
on this fruitless journey to solve her murder.

I was beginning to lose my faith in the police, and
I could now understand why Amanda said we needed
to take things into our own hands.

"We need to go," she said as we sat there. "*Now*.
This waiting is unbearable."

"No." It was May who spoke. She angled her gaze
toward Amanda, fierce and determined. "We can't just
go wandering around the crime scene now. That's an
incredibly stupid idea, Amanda."

"So what? You have a better one?" Amanda's gaze
was sharp.

"What can we do?" May asked, her voice rising with
frustration.

"I don't know—*anything*! Riley didn't kill Kesley.
She was framed, and she's relying on us to get her out
of there."

"Look." May turned to Amanda, almost blocking
Rafe and me and keeping us out of the conversation. "Don't you think that's going to look suspi-
cious? Riley just got arrested for murder. What do
you think is going to happen if people find out we're
missing the next day? Don't you think that makes us
look guilty?"

"I don't *care*," Amanda bit out, her jaw clenched. "I just want Riley out of there."

"You *should* care," May said, her voice sharp.

For a moment, I thought Amanda was going to argue back. The lines around her mouth were tight, and her eyes sparked. But perhaps she understood the logic in what May was saying. She cast me a swift sidelong look and said, "Fine." But the slight twist to her mouth told us she wasn't happy with the decision.

I stared off into the distance, thinking. I still hadn't gathered the courage to tell Diana the truth about where I would be this weekend. Instead, I had patched together a lie about trying to work things out with Lia.

She seemed to believe me, for which I was grateful. With the recent turn of events, she was pretty preoccupied and hadn't questioned me too much. I hated lying to her though. It scared me I could do it so easily. With a few sentences, I could form a story that would lead her to believe something that wasn't true. But lying to her was unavoidable. She'd have forbidden me to go back to the lake, even though the supposed killer was in custody, insisting it would bring back unpleasant memories.

I couldn't help but feel she was right about that.

"Hey, Ava!"

I turned when I heard the sound of my name, and to my surprise, I saw a flash of brown-and-gold curls. I stopped at the end of the cafeteria, where the long corridor led back to the classrooms. Amanda neared, watching me with those hawk-like eyes of hers, but her expression was different. Slightly more open, more unsure, than I was used to.

I stood there awkwardly for a moment. "Can I... help you?"

Amanda rolled her eyes. "No. Well, I wanted to talk about the other night."

"Oh." Surprise colored my voice. *Now* she wanted to talk about it? I shoved my hands into my pockets, staring at a point just over her shoulder. "Okay," I said.

"I've never told anyone about my family before," she said, "apart from Kesley."

I lowered my eyes, unsure of what to tell her. What was I supposed to say to that? "I won't tell anyone, I promise," I told her, realizing what she was getting at. Something seemed to loosen in her face as if relieved, but I didn't think having an alcoholic mother and an absent father was something to be ashamed of.

"Why haven't you told any of the other girls, besides Kesley?" I asked her.

A smile quirked her mouth. "I didn't really want to tell her. She dragged it out of me eventually."

"She does—*did*—that, didn't she?" I said. "She could make you talk about things even when you didn't want to." I felt a surge of emotion well up inside me, a nostalgic feeling that was hard to stem.

Amanda stared at me, her face hard, her jaw tight. Her eyes softened, just slightly, but I still saw it. "Whatever happened to Kesley," she said, "we'll find out."

She said nothing more, just turned and walked away. But as I headed in the direction of my next class, I was smiling.

I sat in Rafe's car parked across from my house and stared down the street.

A family of three was crossing the road, two small girls hanging off their mother's arm. The sight sent a pang of longing through me. It reminded me of the times our foster mother took us to the park when we were younger. She would make sure we all held hands and looked right and then left before crossing. The family of three rounded a bend at the end of the street and disappeared.

"What are you thinking about?"

I turned to look at Rafe. "Kesley," I said honestly. He smiled sadly but didn't say anything. "Do you believe in heaven?" I asked him. "Kesley didn't. She hated that sort of stuff."

"I can't have faith in something I can't see."

I felt a small smile tug at the corners of my mouth. "That's why it's called faith."

He grimaced in response.

"Do you think she would go there?" I asked. "If there was one?"

Rafe looked away from me out the window. "If anyone deserved to go to heaven, it was Kesley."

He leaned over and pressed his lips against my forehead before dropping them lower against the flesh marred by the acid so long ago. I turned to him, feeling those stupid tears sting my eyes. I felt Rafe's fingers brush against my cheek, pushing back the hair that obscured me from his view. I glanced at him. He arched his brows in concern but didn't say anything.

"He'd never touch me there," I whispered.

He smiled a little and said, "I can't imagine why. It's an imperfection. Imperfections make you beautiful."

"Thank you," I whispered, turning away again so he wouldn't see my tears.

When I let myself into the house a few minutes later, my mother was already standing at the door, eyes pinned on Rafe's receding car. Her eyes were narrowed. Her mouth was pressed into a thin line. Suppressed anger.

"Were you *watching* us?" I whispered, face heating.

"No, of course not," she said, but she couldn't look at me.

"Then I guess you already know," I said, seeing through her lie.

My mother turned to look at me, and behind the sadness in her eyes there was something else— suspicion?—that I couldn't place. "Just don't let him hurt you, okay?"

I thought back to the promise he'd made me. "He makes me happy, Mom."

My mother stopped in the motion of closing the door on the cold breeze. She sighed a very motherly sort of sigh and looked at me. "All right, Ava," she said. "But you've been hurt too much in your life already."

I couldn't argue with that.

CHAPTER
Thirteen

SINCE THE ARREST, THERE WAS NO MORE news of Riley.

I wasn't sure whether that was good or not; bail hadn't been granted because of her criminal past and the severity of her alleged crime, so she remained in police custody.

Out of us all, Amanda was taking Riley's arrest the hardest. They'd been close before this, and whenever Riley's name was even mentioned that week, Amanda would demand we travel to Lake O'Hara right away. May or Abbey would calm her down until her glower softened into a scowl, and then she'd sigh heavily and slump back into her seat.

Friday arrived with a flash of lightning and a rumble of thunder. Of all the days it was going to rain, *of course* it had to be today. The access road that twisted and curved up to Lake O'Hara wasn't too challenging, but hiking to the lake wasn't going to be much fun in this weather. I'd been prepared for the cold but not the rain.

I didn't mention this as we all piled into Rafe's car a half hour after school ended and sped off toward the highway. Until we hit the highway, Amanda— who'd only half joked I should ride in the trunk— tapped her foot impatiently every time Rafe stopped for a red light.

Still, I thought this trip was pointless. What would Kesley have thought about all this? Were we just cling- ing to the vain thread of hope we'd find something at the lake?

The car was already packed with everything we needed: clothes, bottles of water, tents, and nonper- ishable foods.

It took more than an hour to reach Yoho National Park. We parked in the Lake O'Hara parking lot, then made our way down the access road. Mountains loomed in the distance, casting deep-blue shadows over the road that mingled with weak rays of yellow light almost instantly smothered by thick, bruise-colored clouds. It was awfully cold outside, made ten times worse by the light drizzle. The road beneath my feet was nothing but gravel and dirt, which squelched as the rain turned the dirt to mud.

We walked in silence up the access road, occasionally walking faster or slower due to the heavy packs we all wore. We were all thinking, thinking, thinking. What would we find at that lake? May spoke to me once, just as we reached the halfway mark to the lake.

"You've done this before, right?" she asked. She was leading the pack, Amanda close behind, but I knew her question was aimed at me.

"Every year since I was ten," I replied. My voice had turned slightly scratchy from not using it for most of the day.

"Aren't there, like, grizzly bears here?" she asked hesitantly. From behind me, Abbey snorted. Apparently, stray bears were the least of her concerns.

I squinted at the trees on either side of us. They were thick and dark and incredibly daunting. Because of the impending storm, the light was dimming quickly. Before I knew it, I wouldn't be able to see my own hands. I hoped we'd reach the camping area before that.

"Mostly in summer," I said to her with a small smile. "The most you'll see are a few elk and maybe some mountain goats if you're lucky."

That was it for conversation. Rafe said nothing the entire way. Even though I knew he liked silence, there was something brooding about his. He was a dark presence that had fallen in step beside me.

The rain intensified, splattering down on us as we crawled toward the lake at a snail's pace. I began to lag behind the others—not because I was worried I might slip and fall but because of the sudden thrumming of nervousness I felt. This wasn't just some spur-of-the-moment camping trip. This was the place where Kesley was *killed*.

Strangled.

Murdered.

The mere thought of the word sent a flaring tightness, almost a pain, through my neck. I closed my eyes, and my fingers flew to my neck. There was nothing there, of course.

My stomach rolled like waves as I remembered it doing in my dream. *That was how Kesley felt before she died*. My legs wobbled, and I took in several deep breaths.

I was not Kesley. I was not being choked. I could breathe. I was alive.

I forced myself to focus on the here and now and peered through the darkness. We had almost reached the lake. Through the night and the rain, I could see that the trees were beginning to thin, the gravel road becoming more exposed. But did I want to go any farther?

No. No, I did not.

Now, seeing that we were drawing closer to the lake, the others were moving more quickly. Rafe stayed beside me.

Something locked me in place and froze my feet together. I *couldn't* move.

"Ava?" Rafe. His voice was soft.

Everyone turned almost simultaneously, eyes flicking from Rafe to me.

"I can't do this," I gasped out. I caught a glimpse of Amanda farther up the pathway. She held the flashlight, highlighting the angry twist of her mouth.

"Get yourself together, Ava," she said. "We're not waiting for you."

Above, the distant rumble of thunder grew louder

until a fork of lightning split the sky. I glanced up at Rafe, and the sudden flash of light illuminated his brilliant blue eyes.

"Rafe, *please*. This is a bad idea," I whispered. He reached for me, curling his hand around my own. The warmth was a small comfort but not enough. There was a chill inside me that not even body heat could vanquish.

Amanda's footsteps crunched ahead of me, fading as the seconds passed, and May hovered just a few paces away, watching us. Abbey was somewhere between the two.

Rafe squeezed my hand. "Just say the word and I'll take you home."

"I…"

"Rafe," said May in a warning tone. "We can't."

I glanced at her. Without the flash of lightning, her face was shrouded in shadow. I thought about what she had just said. *We* can't. Plural. If I left, then they would have to leave too. Suspicion burned in the back of my mind, but I pushed it back. Maybe she was right. I couldn't leave, couldn't give up now.

Not when we were so damn close.

I breathed out a sigh. "Let's go," I said, determined. The path twisted through the trees, and then they parted suddenly, the lake stretching before us.

It was nothing like I remembered.

The smooth surface was broken, interrupted by ripples as the ferocious wind and rain hit it.

In the distance, the mountains rose, dark and impressive.

Panic seized me with its sharp, pointed claws, and my breath caught in my throat. Blackness began to develop at the side of my vision, blotting out the lake. My ears rang as though I had recently been exposed to loud noise. A million memories flooded back to me at that moment: happy, sweet memories. Then sad, grief-filled memories that made me buckle.

My knees slammed into something cold.

A wash of voices sounded from above me—or beside me?—but they seemed far away. I felt myself falling further, unable to stop. And even when I should have hit the ground, should have blacked out, I kept falling, falling, falling…

———

I woke to darkness. It surrounded me, curved around me like a snake.

Something thick and heavy pressed against my eyelids—I was blindfolded. *Blindfolded?* Panic erupted inside me, and I took in an involuntary breath. Or I tried to. Material had been shoved into my mouth like a gag, tasting bitter with mildew. My mind screamed at me to undo the gag and blindfold, but something harsh like rope chafed at my wrists. There was a sharp ache at the back of my head.

I tried to move my feet next, but they too were bound.

Was this it? Was I going to feel a sharp blade at my neck any moment now? Was I living the last seconds of my life? The scream that had built up in my throat died. Had I gotten too close to the truth of Kesley's death? Had the killer come for me next? Ice froze my veins. KARMA was the ones who'd taken me out here. They'd designed this whole plan, and for what? To kill me? Just as I surrendered, something warm touched my forearm. I flinched, but the most I could do was edge my chair a few inches away. It screeched against the floor, sounding wooden.

"It's okay, it's okay," a soft voice murmured from my left.

And then hands were at my mouth and face, pulling off the blindfold and gag. The light slammed into me first, so blinding after such impenetrable darkness that I had to blink several times for anything to come into focus.

I forced myself to breathe slowly, carefully, and assess the situation with a clear mind. It wasn't difficult to recognize KARMA's cabin, but knowing where I was didn't make me feel any better. I remembered walking up to the lake and then...nothing.

So how had I gotten *here*?

I closed my eyes, delved deep into my mind. The throb in the back of my head seemed to intensify, broken images and feelings flashing through my mind. The cold, the wet, the flare of lightning. Arms around me, carrying me forward through the darkness. Voices edged with frustration. The slam of a car door. The sound of an engine revving and rain hitting the windscreen.

I opened my eyes, heart pounding.

"R-Rafe?" I said. My voice was nothing more than a thin whisper.

"I'm here, Ava." I twisted my neck to look at him. The rope and material lay at his feet, but he didn't meet my eyes. He strode to the door and called, "She's awake, Amanda."

The door hung open on its hinges, the *tap-tap-tapping* of rain pummeling against the roof.

Somewhere, a car door slammed. Then I heard squelching footsteps through mud.

"Rafe?" I said again, this time louder. "What happened? How did I get here?"

His voice was unusually clipped when he spoke. "You passed out." My mother had said that too, the day I fainted at the piano.

Rafe said nothing more. Amanda stepped through the door, May and Abbey following close behind her. They were both soaked to the bone, hair dripping water all over the wooden floor. Neither of them seemed to care. May's eyes were puffy and red-rimmed as though she had been crying. Why had she been crying?

"What *happened*?" I yelled.

"Tell her," someone said quietly. May, I think it was. Or maybe Abbey. I didn't know or care.

"Sure thing," said Amanda. There was a sarcastic, biting edge to her voice. She reached for something and threw a bunch of papers on the table before me. Stuck to the papers were a couple newspaper clippings and a paragraph of neat, curvy, and elegant script, handwriting I recognized the moment I laid eyes on it.

It was Kesley's.

"You were six years old. February the eighth, if I'm correct." The date stirred something in the back of my mind, but I couldn't quite reach it. Amanda continued, "It was about, oh, I don't know, three in the afternoon. The roads were coated with a thin layer of ice that was gradually melting. They were slippery, very slippery. Your father was driving you home from school when a truck hit your car."

February eighth. A date I'd never forget.

"Your father died instantly. But thank God for children's seats, eh? 'Cause you survived. Afterward, you were diagnosed with post-traumatic stress disorder. Obviously. You say you can't remember much of your life when you were young, don't you? Well, there's why. Your brain erased those memories for you because you couldn't cope with them. You missed your father, Ava. But you were lucky; you escaped with nothing but a few scrapes and bruises."

"I know this!" I yelled. A familiar aching started inside my chest, threatening to tear me up from the inside out.

Amanda didn't say anything for a moment. She just looked at me, eyes pitiless as she watched the tears fall down my cheeks. She leaned over and pulled a sheet of paper from the desk and held it out for me to see.

I had to blink a few times so the tears didn't blur my vision.

It looked like medical records of some sort. In the

top right-hand corner of the paper was a name. *Evelyn Hale*. My mother's name. And on the left-hand side, *Circling Pines Mental Health Clinic*. Oh God, hadn't someone broken into the clinic not that long ago and stolen patient medical information? My stomach roiled. I blinked several more times, the documents becoming clearer. I skimmed the paper, unsure of what Amanda wanted me to see. It was a medical list of my mother's many previous conditions. Someone had highlighted the top one in bright pink.

Chronic depression, it read.

I cleared my throat before I spoke. "My mother killed herself."

"We know." There was no mistaking the unforgiving edge to Amanda's tone. Her eyes flashed as she bent down toward me. "What else do you remember about back then?"

I squeezed my eyes shut, hoping that would stem the tears, but they continued their steady path down my cheeks. "Darkness," I answered in a whisper. "That's all I remember."

I felt her hand wrap around my wrist. Tight. Painfully so. "Think," Amanda snarled. "*Think*, Ava." But there was nothing. Nothing but swirling darkness, as thick and as impenetrable as a concrete wall.

"I can't. *I can't*. How can I remember something when there's nothing there?"

I heard Amanda breathe in a deep breath of frustration. I opened my eyes.

She said, "You saw it."

There was a pause.

"I-I saw what?"

"You saw your mother kill herself." My heart beat faster; my stomach contracted and then heaved as though I was going to be sick.

"No…no, I…don't remember," I whispered. "How do you know any of this? You're lying. You have to be lying."

"Kesley" was Amanda's simple answer, though it meant no sense to me.

"*What?*"

"Kesley told us. She told us everything. The summer after your father died, your mother suggested it would be best for you to head up to your grandmother's. She was old, you know. And your mom said she wanted you and Kesley to spend some time with her before she died. But really, she wanted to be alone. You refused to go. So it was just you and your mother, alone at home while Kesley stayed in Vancouver for a month.

"You weren't supposed to be home, Ava. You were

supposed to be in day care for the morning—you know that one just down the street from your house? Yeah, well, you didn't like it there apparently. You slipped through the back gates an hour before your mother was supposed to pick you up for the day. It wasn't far from where you lived, so you were able to find your way back home—"

"*I can't remember any of this!*"

"I'm getting to that, bitch," snarled Amanda. Her fingers trembled, and she raised her hand.

"Amanda, *no*—" I heard Rafe yell out from somewhere behind me, but it was already too late. Amanda threw back her hand and swung it forward, slapping me across the face. Hard. My head snapped to the side, tears of pain stinging the back of my eyes. I breathed in deeply, trying to ignore the stinging on my right cheek.

"That wasn't *necessary*," Rafe said through gritted teeth.

"Speak for yourself," Amanda muttered. Silence fell, and nobody seemed willing to break it. My cheek stung, and the places where the rope had cut into my wrists and ankles burned.

Amanda leaned against the wall. As far from me as she could get. "Your mother was chronically depressed,

Ava, so she took herself from the world. You were
there, waiting, just outside your kitchen where your
mother was. She had a knife in her hand."

A blade raised high. Light pouring from the window.
A voice: frail, unsure, broken, saying, "Ava. Go. Please,
just go!" And then…blackness.

A flashback I'd had before. A *flashback*. Now I knew
it for what it was. Not a dream, not a nightmare.

I pressed my eyes closed. The aching in my chest
had intensified like fire. "I don't want to hear any
more of this, Amanda," I said. "Please, *stop*."

She continued like I hadn't spoken. "She stabbed
herself—right there and then. I guess you could say
you were at the wrong place, wrong time." Her mouth
twisted into an ugly expression I couldn't decipher.
"And you saw *everything*." She placed a heavy emphasis on the last word, and it sent a shiver down my spine.
I was glad I couldn't fully remember that part.

"And do you know what happened next?" said
Amanda.

"No, Amanda, I don't," I said in a flat voice.

"You stayed there."

"Stayed where?"

"Beside your mother's body."

My mouth went dry. "Why?"

Amanda's lips quivered, and for the first time, I saw a flicker of something sympathetic dance across her face. "You were waiting for her to wake. Only she didn't wake. The day care was freaking out. They called the police, and they found you there that afternoon. You told them, 'Just one minute, she'll be awake then. Just one more minute.' Only she wasn't. And then Kesley came back. She asked you what happened, and you told her."

I stared blankly at the wall behind Amanda. I didn't say anything.

I didn't have anything to say. Amanda told me how Kesley thought she had it worse because she could remember our parents—but God, she hadn't been through half the shit I had. Amanda was staring at me with an intently piercing gaze. "You still don't get it, do you?"

"Get what?" I asked.

"She was angry! She was so, so angry! She blamed you for your mother's death! Don't you get it? You. Were. There. You could have stopped it. You spent hours sitting beside your mother's dead body as it decomposed, thinking she was just sleeping! If you'd done something, anything, she could probably still be alive!"

"I was *six*," I yelled at her, so, so close to tears. "How could she have *blamed* me for something I can't even remember?"

"I don't know," Amanda whispered, her voice harsh, "but she certainly found a way."

"What's that supposed to mean?"

Amanda said nothing. She came closer and traced a finger across the scar on the left side of my face. What she was saying without words slammed into me.

A choked sob sounded in the cabin. A sound that came from me.

Amanda opened her mouth and started to speak once more. This time, I didn't need to hear what she was telling me. The truth sat in front of me, and for the first time in my life, it was so close that I could touch it. And I didn't want it.

It wasn't an accident like I thought—like everyone thought.

Kesley. It was all Kesley. How had she done it and looked into my face every single day, seeing what she'd done? Had throwing a jar of hydrofluoric acid in my face been worth it? For something I couldn't even *remember*?

I thought back to that day—to the blurry images I'd managed to grasp before they slipped through my fingers. There was pain, a lot of pain, the sound of hurried footsteps, harsh voices, the sound of sirens… The more I tried to focus on each individual sound or thought, the further it slipped away.

"But my mother?" I asked breathlessly. And then I added, "My foster mother?"

Amanda glanced over at May, who nodded.

May said very quietly, "She knew what Kesley had done."

"But—"

"She told the paramedics it was an accident. You were supposed to be waiting for Diana in the waiting room where you were allowed, and you, Ava, wandered into an unlocked room. She said you must have been tampering with the jars."

I felt my face crumple. "She…she lied? For Kesley?"

Amanda wrapped her arms around her chest. She looked tired, like she wanted all this to be done. She wasn't the only one, I thought.

"She lied to protect Kesley," Abbey said, finally speaking.

"Kesley never told me this," I said numbly. "She never told me the truth."

"But did she ever tell you the truth, Ava?" Abbey asked.

"There were a lot of things Kesley never told you," Amanda said.

"Why are you *defending* her?" I asked in a hoarse whisper. I didn't look up.

To my surprise, it wasn't Amanda who answered. May, who was still in the farthest corner of the cabin, replied. She said, her voice flat, "Because she's dead, Ava. There's nobody left to defend her."

"What has any of this got to do with Kesley's murder?" I asked, heart pounding.

Silence had fallen as soon as I opened my mouth. They all looked at each other, and I understood that *this* was the question they were prepared for.

The question they were terrified of.

"Everything," said Amanda softly. "We... Rafe, what are you doing?" Someone was at my shoulder. Something cold cut into my arm, but as I gasped and looked down, I saw that Rafe was only cutting the ropes that tied me down.

"*Rafe, stop.*" Amanda's voice was firm.

"She's not going to hurt anyone," Rafe said calmly, bending down to free my ankles. The cold air stung my skin as the rope sprung away. I glanced at Rafe, catching a glimpse of his eyes for a few moments before he turned away.

He didn't look at me.

"*She* won't," spat Amanda. *She?* Who—me? "I knew you wouldn't be able to do this properly. I just knew it!"

"I'm *handling* it," Rafe almost snarled. "Kesley trusted me more than you, so just shut up, won't you?"

Amanda laughed, and it was a bitter, humorless sound. "Yeah, you're right. She probably did. But she didn't count on you falling in love with her sister."

A steely silence filled the cabin, and Amanda took advantage of the quiet to yank some sheets of paper out of the pile sitting in front of me.

"What's that?" I asked, my voice dry and thin.

"Proof."

I took the proffered papers with shaking hands. They'd been printed from various websites. Some paragraphs were highlighted, circled, underlined. Others had notes scrawled in the margins, and sections had been cut out and glued onto pages.

"I don't…I don't understand." The sheets of paper were limp, loose in my hands.

But at the same time, I was terrified to let go. They were my anchor. If I let them go, just for a moment, I would go hurtling into a cold abyss.

Though maybe that was where I was headed anyway.

"You don't *understand?*" Amanda turned. She walked right up to me and bent down slowly until we were eye to eye. "Fine. Let me spell it out for you." She paused. When she continued, she pronounced every word with careful, knifelike precision. "You. Killed. Kesley. And now an innocent girl is in custody because of *you.*"

CHAPTER

Fourteen

"I-I DON'T UNDERSTAND," I SAID WEAKLY.
Then, "No. *No*. I don't believe—"

I let my eyes drop to the papers in my hand.

Dissociative Identity Disorder, said the title. I trailed my fingers across the page, feeling the rough edges where handwritten notes had been stuck down with tape. Everything was neat, ordered, precise. These were Kesley's notes—I recognized her handwriting. Phrases jumped out at me from the pages: "traumatic events," "under the age of nine," "memory loss," "traumatic memories split off," "formation of additional personalities," "a feeling of detachment or surreality." The words continued on and on and on until I couldn't read anymore. Until the tears that had been forming in my eyes became so thick that they obscured my vision. A frisson of fear passed through me like an icy-cold breeze on a winter's night.

"You still don't believe it? *Here*."

And she slammed something down on the table. It was her school laptop. Her fingers shook as she pressed the On button and the screen glowed to life.

"Watch," snarled Amanda. "And describe to me what you see."

For a moment, everything on screen was dark. All I heard was the hiss of rain slamming against the lake and the quiet murmuring of voices. They were too soft to make out any clear words. Then beams of light sliced through the darkness. *The moon?* No, it was still raining. Flashlights.

Someone was lying on the ground, blond hair catching the light. *Oh God.* My stomach swooped. That was *me*. I twisted around in my seat, searching for Rafe, but he stared blankly out the window.

I turned to the screen. The rain was beginning to cease, but the *drip-drip* of water still fell from the pine trees. My figure, small and vulnerable-looking, twitched on the ground before a sudden audible gasp came from my lips and I sat up.

I did not look like me.

It *was* me. That was my caramel-colored hair, my dark eyes, my slightly rounded shoulders, and my scarred, twisted face. I was streaked with dirt; it smudged under my eyes like makeup. And still, even though I knew it was me, subtle things told another story, things that didn't look quite right.

The cold, almost cruel twist of my mouth—beyond the scarring of my face. The sharpness of my eyes. Even the way I held myself looked different. My chin was tilted slightly higher, more defiantly, more *confidently*.

"Hey, bitch!" The voice came from the trees. Although the camera quality was poor, I could tell it was Amanda. Her tall, sharp figure was illuminated by the flashlight.

My figure jerked away from the bright light, eyes narrowed.

I didn't remember waking up in the trees, only the cabin. Everything else was blank. Completely, utterly, and terrifyingly blank.

I stared at the screen and watched myself glaring at Amanda.

"You know that's not my name," I—*she*—said.

"Whatever. I think it suits you just fine. Now, tell me, why you killed Kesley, Margo?" Though her voice was as harsh and cruel as it always was, her shaking hands betrayed her fear. I—Margo?—got to my feet.

"Don't," said Amanda, and she backed up, yanking something from her pocket. The metallic surface glinted in the light. A gun.

Margo's eyes narrowed skeptically. "I bet you don't even know how to use one of those."

There was a click as Amanda flicked off the safety switch. "Oh yeah? You want to bet on that? How about if I can't shoot you, you go free, and if I do know how to shoot, you die?"

A voice came from the darkness: Rafe. "I swear to God, Amanda, if you shoot her—"

"Shut up." Amanda's voice was so vicious that Rafe said nothing else.

Margo eyed the gun, not moving an inch. Amanda's threat was deadly real to her—and me. "You took me here. You flushed me out."

"We thought this would be the best place, eh? Brings back a lot of memories, doesn't it?" Anger sharpened Amanda's voice into the edge of a knife. "Like when you murdered Kesley."

"She deserved it." Margo's voice lowered to a snarl,

every syllable shaking with rage. "I hope she rots in hell until she's reduced down to ash. Can't you see? Everyone thinks *I'm* the bad one here. But do you know what it's like to have a rope tied around your neck until you're right there—right at the point of death—over and over again? Do you know how much I wished Kesley would just end it? But that bitch drew it out. All for something Ava couldn't control." There was a whimper from behind the camera, and it sounded like Abbey.

A low sob ripped from my throat. Here I was—only it wasn't really *me*—confessing to the murder of the person that, despite everything, I had loved most in the world.

Margo continued, "And you know what the best part of all this is? She knew it was me, long before I killed her. She figured everything out to the last goddamn detail. And I swear to God, I enjoyed squeezing the last seconds of her life from her."

Amanda's fingers shook on the gun. "Shut up or I swear on Kesley's grave I will shoot you."

"Stop it! Just stop it!" It was May who had screamed from the shadows somewhere to the left of the camera.

"Shoot me?" said Margo. "Go ahead, but you'll be shooting Ava too. Shooting poor, vulnerable Ava."

"I don't care—" And Amanda pulled the trigger. Someone crashed into the side of her just as a bullet blasted through the air, narrowly missing Margo's head. She flinched away from the shot, which instead embedded itself in the tree behind her.

Amanda struggled with whoever had thrown her to the ground, but they were much stronger than she was. "You promised, Rafe!" she half gasped, half yelled.

"I know, and I'm going to stick to that promise—"

"Let me up!" she yelled, eyes widening. "She killed Kesley! Your best friend!"

"I know, I *know*!" Rafe yelled. "I promised Kesley we'd find out the truth behind Margo. Just give me a moment—"

"A moment? Jesus, you choose *this* moment to hesitate? We've been planning this since she died! I *told you* not to get close to her. *I told you!*"

"Your plans never included killing her!"

Amanda launched forward and slammed the butt of the gun into the side of Margo's head. I watched as my figure crumpled to the floor.

"Stop it," I said. I dragged my eyes away from the laptop screen. "Turn it off. I don't want to see any more."

Amanda switched the video off, eyes leaking tears

she didn't try to stop. The screen in front of me flickered and fell to black.

I felt empty, cold.

So there it was. The truth I'd been searching for since Kesley's death. And although the truth can set one free, it also holds the power to destroy them. This one just might.

Because everything, *everything*, came apart at that moment.

No longer would I be able to walk down the street without people staring at me.

No longer could I garner smiles from passersby.

No longer was I that innocent girl, that one whose sister was murdered.

Oh, how I'd wished I wouldn't always be *that girl whose sister was brutally murdered*. Seemed as though I had gotten my wish. Now I was *that girl who killed her sister*.

The girl who people skirted around in the streets.

A killer, a criminal, a murderer.

Me.

"I-I killed... But Kesley..." I couldn't get the words out. They stuck in my throat like superglue, tight and uncomfortable.

I heard soft footfalls from behind me, and a warm

hand brushed over the scarred side of my cheek and down my neck where the scars extended.

"Kesley believed in…" Rafe paused, searching for the right words. "Retribution. That when someone did something wrong, something equally bad would happen to them."

"Karma," I said almost robotically.

Rafe continued, not showing that he'd heard what I said. "She wanted to hurt you as bad as you hurt her. So she…" He hesitated, and for the first time tonight, I heard a flicker of emotion color his tone. "She…"

He couldn't finish. I still didn't look at him. I didn't want to see his expression.

My stomach twisted, but I still said, "She did what?"

"She choked you," Abbey said. My eyes flickered to her face, which was blank and emotionless, apart from the tears that leaked from her eyes. "She locked you in her wardrobe and choked you over and over again."

How had I not *known*? I touched my cheek, my throat, my neck. And because the scars from the acid extended down and wrapped around my neck, I'd never noticed the extra mutilation from the rope.

I closed my eyes and felt hot tears slide down my cheek just as another suppressed memory fought its way to the surface.

The rope around my neck grew tighter, tighter. I couldn't breathe. I could hardly see. But a flash of color danced across my vision—ribbons of blond, silky hair. I struggled against the rope, but the more I struggled, the more the rope was tightened. Was I going to die this time?

I jolted back to the present, but when I glanced down at the sweater I wore, I was pulled under by another vivid, warped memory.

Diana, my new mother, straightened the turtleneck sweater and smiled at me. Looking at myself in the mirror, the bruises and scabs were completely covered. "Don't tell anyone, okay, sweetie? Your sister didn't mean to. She's very sorry."

I looked over my shoulder in the reflection.

Kesley stood there.

She didn't look very sorry.

But my memories were so scattered. Fragments, shards of things—thoughts, feelings—rattled inside me like loose coins.

I stood before the mirror, alone. The rough, bloodied skin of my neck was healing now, but even so, it ached. And ached. And ached. Sometimes, late at night when the moon shone brightly in the sky, I'd sit up in bed unable to breathe.

Sometimes, Kesley was there; sometimes, it was my imagination.

Eventually, the bruises had faded enough to blend into the disfigurement left over from the acid. My brain had suppressed the awful, awful memories, and I had been none the wiser.

Until now.

My *own sister* had abused me. Choked me until I teetered on the brink of death and then started all over again—all because of something I couldn't even remember. All the guilt, all the pity evaporated right then and there, replaced with burning hatred. Maybe she deserved what she had gotten after all.

Karma it truly was.

I'd felt sorry for her. No, scratch that. I'd felt heartbroken that I'd been so blind to her sadness. That night when I had seen the noose in her wardrobe, I thought that had been for *her*. Oh, how wrong I'd been.

I raised my head slowly to look at Amanda. Hot tears dripped from my eyes, and for once, I didn't care.

They knew. For how long?

"When you said you didn't have a chance to talk to Kesley before she died," I said to Rafe, "you lied, didn't you?"

He nodded.

"What happened? When you came back?"

Rafe took a deep breath, then said, "I came back to Circling Pines, and Kesley asked to meet at the park the day before she died. KARMA was there. That was when I found about her involvement in that—I swear, Ava. I didn't know before that. I didn't know anything before that. She told us what we know now and gave us her notes. She told us she was beginning to notice things in you for a couple years. An expression in your eye or the way you'd walk or the way you'd dress. Once she realized she might be in danger because of what she did… I tried reasoning with her, telling her she was jumping to wild conclusions." Rafe's eyes grew wet with tears. "That's when she told us about the abuse. About what she did to you. None of us *wanted* to believe it."

"That's what tonight was about," Abbey whispered. "We had to make sure."

Then why all this? Why put me through all this?

"The…police," I said, taking great, gasping breaths between each word. "Why not go straight to the police?"

"You think any of us wanted to *believe* you killed your own *sister?*" May cried. "Is *that* what you wanted? For us—for *Rafe*—to turn our backs on you?" I didn't want to think of Rafe. Not now, not anytime soon. "All we had were Kesley's notes and what she told us. We…we knew from the files we stole from the hospital that what she claimed about your mother was true but not anything else." Her voice trembled. "What Kesley did was *horrible*. I don't know *why* she did what she did. We're not trying to hurt you, Ava. We're trying to *help* you."

I stood, and I didn't realize I was moving until I was right in front of Rafe. His eyes cut to mine. I couldn't read the expression in his eyes.

"So you lied to me," I whispered. "When I asked you if you knew that someone was after Kesley. Did you know it was me? All along?"

He didn't say anything. Perhaps he couldn't find the right words, because he just nodded. The sickening feeling in my stomach intensified.

How had he fallen for a *killer*? Had it all been faked?

Part of me, the weak part, wanted to run. And keep on running. Because there was a kind of bliss in running from your problems. But no, I was sick of running. For the first time in my life, I was going battle through.

I stared unseeingly at the floor. "That's why she didn't tell me anything," I said, more to myself than the others. I looked at Rafe, daring him to contradict me. "I was right. She didn't trust me. Just not for the reasons I first thought."

Of course she wouldn't tell me a thing. Especially not if she suspected me. But then…

"Then that's why she made KARMA," I said, flinging my words at Amanda. "She knew what she'd done to me. What she'd caused. So she created a trail to make sure, again, that I got what I deserved. She *used* you."

I realized a moment later that I shouldn't have said that.

Amanda's face had gone utterly blank. And her voice was deadly cold when she said, "How *dare* you?"

Kesley dragged them into this mess.

Call me a bitch, a monster, for all the things I had done—but was Kesley any better? They didn't deserve any of this. Least of all Rafe. She snared them in her games because she was afraid. Afraid that her death was going to become an unsolved mystery.

Amanda turned her back on me. And I realized I'd *completely* underestimated her. She had been willing to die for Kesley. How would Kesley have felt knowing that? Such loyalty.

She really had them wrapped around her little finger, didn't she?

"I'm sorry," I whispered. It was the best I could do. But it was pitifully inadequate.

"I think we're all a little bit sorry," May whispered. Tears shone in her eyes. For me? For Kesley? For all of us?

"You're *sorry*?" Amanda said. "You murdered your own sister, and you're *sorry*? Kesley might have done some terrible things but that doesn't mean she deserved to *die* for them."

"Ava needs our *help*, Amanda," Rafe yelled. He ran his hand roughly through his hair. Amanda opened her mouth, maybe about to say something, but Rafe said, "I don't *care* what you say next to defend Kesley. I. Don't. Fucking. Care. There is *nothing* you could say that would change what she did to her sister."

Silence fell. "Easy for you to say," she snarled.

Rafe's eyes widened in disbelief. "How has any of this been easy on me? Don't delude yourself into thinking you're the only one this is affecting!"

Amanda said, "Don't say I didn't warn you. She's nothing like Kesley was."

"You're right," I said fiercely. "I am *nothing* like Kesley was. And you know what? I wanted to be. I wanted to be that girl who was talented and pretty and had everything, but she was so, so much more than that, wasn't she? I never wanted to be the girl she really was."

"Guys, guys," said May. "We're not getting anywhere here, okay?" As she glanced at me, I saw an emotion I'd never seen when people looked at me before: fear. May was actually scared of me. But was Kesley? In those final weeks of her life, had she been afraid of me? Was she worried I would finally snap and…and…do what I did?

If she was, she gave nothing away.

"You're right," Amanda said. "We're not getting anywhere. Yet."

Something in her words sent a flurry of fear through me. What did she mean? I didn't have time to look for hidden meanings.

Rafe spoke, and his voice was almost pleading. I'd never heard him sound that desperate before. "Amanda, please, we should think about this properly…"

"*Think* about this?" There was a cutting edge of anger in her voice. "I've thought about this ever since the day Kesley *died*. Ever since I went into school that day and saw everyone's expressions, and I just *knew*."

"God, please, there has to be another way—"

"I said *no*!" she yelled. Her eyes were wild, fists clenched, and I thought she might hit me, but she only threw a glance at the door. Was she expecting someone? "You're not backing out now. You just *can't*. You know I *told you* not to get involved, and you promised you could keep your head. And now..." She drew in a sharp, angry breath.

I hated to ask him. But I did. "Then why...why get so close to me in the first place?"

It wasn't Rafe that answered.

"Because he just couldn't help himself," Amanda said from behind me. I turned. She was standing very close, an intense expression shadowing the features of her face, as if she were shutting off her emotions. "I told him he couldn't get emotionally attached, that it would only end badly for him, but he didn't listen."

Something in her words made me stiffen. "End... badly?" *End badly, end badly, end badly...*

It clicked.

I stumbled back, hitting the wall. There was nowhere else to go. Cold dread wove around me, binding me to the spot. The sound of fast-approaching sirens cut through the air, their wailing screech becoming louder and louder with each passing moment.

I shrank back into the corner. "No," I whispered. "No, *please, no*. Please, I won't—"

I broke off. I won't *what*? Hurt any more people?

How could I control something I simply wasn't in control of?

"I'm sorry, Ava," May said. "But we owe Kesley. We all owe Kesley."

I remembered what I'd thought at the lookout point. Everything was a circle; it all ended back at Kesley, no matter what. Would this be the end of it all? Would I begin to heal after this?

Could I ever heal?

I shrank back into the corner, letting my matted hair fall across my face.

"Someone get her outside," a voice said. I didn't know who.

"No," I said, whipping my head back around. I knew what I must look like: eyes wide, damp hair framing my face. *Crazy.* But wasn't I? I couldn't let this happen. I was going to do everything in my power to stop it in its tracks. "Kesley wouldn't want this to happen. She wouldn't. I know it!"

May and Abbey both flinched.

Amanda leveled a glance my way. "You were right before, you know. About Kesley using us, 'cause I guess in a twisted way she was. But I don't care about that, Ava. She brought me out of a place I couldn't get free from. I owe her so much. We promised Kesley we'd bring her death to justice." She walked forward and grabbed my arm, her grip like iron, and tried to pull me from the room.

I held back with all the strength I could.

I looked around the cabin until I met Rafe's eyes. He was watching with an expression I couldn't decipher as Amanda tried to haul me outside.

"Was *everything* a lie?" I asked him.

His lips parted in surprise. Just a moment ago, fear had curved through every syllable I spoke, but now my voice was calm.

"It was real, I swear," he said softly. I sucked in a breath of the cold night air that wafted through the open door. "But I can't protect you, Ava. You have to go to the police—"

"No!" I yanked my arm from Amanda's grip. "Rafe—you said nothing was going to hurt me. You *promised* me!"

The sirens were deafening now. The windows reflected the blinking red-and-blue lights, the glass turning purple where they threaded together. The unified sound of slamming doors came from outside. The shouts of policemen sounded warped and distant, like I was hearing them from underwater.

All four walls of the cabin felt like they were closing

in on me, threatening to swallow me whole. There was only one thing left I could do, even though every particle of my body screamed against me, willing me to turn away from all this.

I was a weak person.

I strived for the easiest, least frightening way of getting through life. I didn't take risks. I didn't do foolish things. I sought comfort from my sister when she was alive and from Rafe when she wasn't. But in that moment, I did the bravest, strongest thing I'd ever done.

I stepped outside into the waiting arms of the police.

This, Kesley, is how our tragedy ended. With snow drifting outside and piling against my barred windows.

Time passes strangely when you are in a mental hospital. At the beginning, everything was a blur, but as the days lengthened into a month and then two, my life settled into a routine.

I woke. I took my medication. I saw my therapist.

My mind was split, tainted by crimes that would never wash away. No matter how many apologies I uttered, no matter what drugs they hooked me on, she'd always be there. Lurking like a black shadow, waiting, waiting. Waiting to uncoil herself from my mind. That bitter girl who'd stood up to you for those awful things you did to me, the one who lured you to the lake to choke you.

Margo, they'd said her name was. Such a pretty, innocent name. But all she had been was a suppressed emotion. A cold, coiling fear that had blossomed into defiance. And with that defiance had come a spark that caught fire and destroyed a life. Your life.

Margo was brought out during hypnosis and psychotherapy, where my psychotherapist encouraged us to coexist. To fuse together. It was never about destroying her—as much as I wanted her gone. Margo was, for better or worse, a part of me.

I was told later that Margo confessed to killing Kesley not only for the things she'd done to me but also because she'd been getting close to the truth about Margo. Margo had taken root in my mind and wanted to stay there.

My therapist suggested I try painting again. She thought that, like writing this letter, it might help purge some of the terrible thoughts in my mind. She told me it could be used as a safe way for Margo to let herself be heard.

Eventually, I was allowed visitors. That was the hardest part. Our mother—I can only think of her as Diana now—came first. A case had been opened against her, and she had been found guilty of child neglect. She was allowed to see me with strict supervision after entering a plea bargain, pending my therapist's and my own approval.

She'd perched on the edge of my bed and stared at me the first time, not speaking. So I did. "Why did you lie for her? Cover for her? I don't understand."

She opened her mouth but didn't say anything.

"She hurt me," I said. "Your daughter. In more

ways than one." I could feel the anger rising again, but I shoved it viciously down. If I got angry, the orderlies would come and restrain me. They'd done it before, when I first came here. I didn't remember any of it, so it must've been Margo.

When the anger came, she came with it.

"I'm sorry," Diana said, and tears dripped steadily down her cheeks. "I thought... I didn't realize how bad things had gotten, Ava. Not until it was too late. I didn't think it would amount to all this." She waved her hand around my room a little hopelessly. "So many times, I thought of... of doing something—but what could I do? Go to the police? They would have taken you and Kesley away from me. You know I always wanted children. Always. But no matter how hard I tried, I couldn't get pregnant. I just couldn't. So I chose foster care. Then I found you and Kesley, and you were perfect. And then Kesley...she did that terrible, horrible thing, and I just...I didn't know what to do. How was I to choose between my children? What was right and what was wrong? It all stopped before your seventh birthday. I thought maybe, maybe with time you would forget. You were so young. I'm sorry, Ava. I'm so sorry."

"Sometimes," I said, "sorry isn't good enough."

"Maybe one day," she said softly, "it will be."

I hoped she was right.

What she did—did that make her a terrible person? Or just a broken, confused person? She could have gotten you help. She could have done something instead of watching me suffer. She didn't have to turn her back and pretend that nothing was wrong in her fairy tale life, and she didn't have to live in denial. But life, I realized, wasn't made up of rights or wrongs—only choices that define who you are. Decisions were blurry, often contorted with personal emotion. You might have been the one to start it all. But Diana let it happen.

And I will always, always resent her for that.

I find myself taking a lot of comfort in books. They help to quiet Margo. Besides, books have always kept me company in a way people couldn't.

After the arrest, there was enough evidence for the police to search my house. Hidden under the floorboards beneath my bed was a box of things I had no recollection of putting there: clothes, newspaper clippings, bloodied pieces of rope, watches...and that note I'd found hidden in the

piano. Margo had put it there, I now und
when I "passed out" or switched personalit...

She'd been the one to plant evidence against
Riley too.

Lia came soon after my therapist thought it
would be beneficial to reconnect with old friends,
but she only stood awkwardly at the door and
looked at me as though I were a ghost. She'd come
hand in hand with Jackson. He could barely look
me in the eye without flinching.

They haven't come again.

I don't blame them. How must it feel, finding
out you dated a killer and had no idea about it?

And Kesley... I know how it feels to think you
know someone, only to have what you thought was
true turned upside down and inside out.

My only other visitor is Rafe. I didn't want to
see him for a long time, and it was even longer
until my therapist helped me understand that
avoiding him wasn't helping me. "You can run
away from your problems," she'd said, "or you can
face them head-on. It will never be as bad as you
think it will."

So the next day, when Rafe came, I let him in.

"Hi," he said.

"Hey." It was hard to get the word out.

"Can I sit?"

"If you want." I watched him take a seat on my bed. I was sitting in the old, moth-eaten chair in the corner of the room, my legs curled underneath me, with a book in my lap. I found it hard to look at him. But Rafe had his bright-blue eyes focused carefully on me, watching. Perhaps to see if Margo was there. She wasn't.

The longer I took the medication and the more psychotherapy I had, the less I felt her, so to speak. Sometimes, in times of stress or vivid emotion, I felt her lying curled up somewhere in the back of my mind like she was sleeping. Other times I'd wake from a terrible, breathless memory, and I could feel her like a physical presence, telling me to do bad things. When that happened, I closed my eyes and focused my breathing until she fell away. Now it is happening less and less.

That first time Rafe came, things were strained. No, more than strained. How could I ever forgive him for what he had done to me? I told him, "I don't know why you're here."

For a moment, I thought he wouldn't answer. Then he said, "Because I care about you."

"If you cared about me, then you would have just told me the truth."

"If we told you what we knew, what would you have done?" Rafe said, and I looked up to meet his eyes. They were sad, conflicted. I thought about what he was saying.

"I don't know," I said honestly.

"Yes, exactly." His words were blunt, but his voice was soft. He stretched out his hand as if reaching for mine, but I flinched, and he dropped his hand. I looked away as he said, "I've told you this before, but Kesley was like a sister to me. I would have done anything for her. Anything. But once I found out what she'd did to you, Ava... God, I'm sorry. I'm so, so sorry. I didn't want to believe any of it. I didn't want to believe she could do something so terrible. All I wanted was the truth and for you to begin to heal." He blinked away tears. "And I didn't believe what she'd done—not fully—until I saw Margo that night."

"Do you think she loved me?" I whispered. "At all?"

"I don't know, Ava. I don't know."

I said nothing to that. Just cried.

He's come every day I've been allowed visitors

since then. The good days and the bad. Sometimes, Margo was so present in me that I couldn't remember those days, but he did, and on occasion, I caught him looking at me with an almost haunted expression in his eyes. I still couldn't truly find it in myself to forgive him. Not yet anyway.

But he cared for me, and I cared for him.

One day, when my mind was plagued with flashbacks and emotions buried deep, deep, deep in my mind, Rafe came into my room. Without saying anything, he knew it was a bad day.

He reached for my hand, and this time, I let him take it.

So that's it, Kesley. Our story splayed out in a notebook in front of me, but I think we both know it doesn't end here. Will it ever end? Maybe, maybe not. Because I know that even at my last breath, all three of us will be there: you, me, and Margo.

Right until the very end.

Love eternally,

Ava.

Acknowledgments

For someone who's been dreaming of having her novel published since she was twelve, I now find myself rendered rather speechless. Nevertheless, here we go!

First and foremost, to Wattpad. Without you, none of this would've been possible. The work you guys do is incredible. Thank you, thank you, thank you. To all my readers who commented and gave me endless encouragement—thank you. Every comment made my day that much brighter, and this novel might not be here without you.

To the incredible team at Sourcebooks, especially

Aubrey Poole and Kate Prosswimmer, who always knew how to make Ava Hale's story better. Thanks for taking a chance on me.

Thanks to Diane Dannenfeldt and my production editor, Elizabeth Boyer, for pointing out my (sometimes embarrassingly obvious) errors.

Thank you to my amazing parents, Coralie and Milton, for always believing in me—even when I didn't. Thanks for putting up with me, and sorry for all the gray hairs I've caused over the years. To Rhys and Andrea, for all the love and support. Rhys, you're the best big brother I could've asked for. To Jo, John, Wilson (Look, Wilson, you're in a book—once you're older, you'll realize how truly epic that is!), and Lin, whose enthusiasm never failed to warm me. To Grandpa and Darleen, for your endless excitement and love. Grandpa: your tidbits and stories inspire me more than you can possibly realize. To Alex and Narelle, for the encouragement and the support. Alex, you're going to be a wonderful teacher. To my godmother, Rea: your kindness, generosity, and support make me want to be a better person. Thank you.

To Helen and John Terzis. Wherever you are now, I hope you're proud of me.

To Nataysia, talented writer and even better friend—
thank you. I'm very grateful to call you my friend.

And finally—thank you to anyone reading this.
Thanks for giving this book a chance.

About the Author

Kara Terzis was twelve when she wrote her first novel and hasn't stopped writing since. Later she started publishing her work on Wattpad, where in 2013 she won the Sourcebooks Story Development Prize, leading to the publication of her debut novel, *Frayed*. She adores fairy tales, photography, rainy days, and film sound tracks. When she's not writing, you can find her buried in a good book and daydreaming. She lives with her family in Sydney, Australia.